U0132738

卓越系列

教育部高职高专油气工程类教指委推荐教材

热能与动力工程专业英语

主 编 胡月红

天津大学出版社
TIANJIN UNIVERSITY PRESS

图书在版编目(CIP)数据

热能与动力工程专业英语/胡月红主编. —天津:天津
大学出版社,2008.3
ISBN 978 - 7 - 5618 - 2631 - 7

Ⅰ. 热… Ⅱ. 胡… Ⅲ. ①热能-英语-高等学校:技术
学校-教材②动力工程-英语-高等学校:技术学校一
教材 Ⅳ. H31

中国版本图书馆 CIP 数据核字(2008)第 022677 号

出版发行	天津大学出版社
出 版 人	杨欢
地　　址	天津市卫津路 92 号天津大学内(邮编:300072)
电　　话	发行部:022—27403647　邮购部:022—27402742
印　　刷	廊坊市长虹印刷有限公司
经　　销	全国各地新华书店
开　　本	169mm×239mm
印　　张	8.5
字　　数	236 千
版　　次	2008 年 3 月第 1 版
印　　次	2008 年 3 月第 1 次
印　　数	1—2 000
定　　价	18.00 元

前　言

近年来,随着国民经济的增长,我国能源动力领域发展迅速,大多数工作岗位的技术含量越来越高,对操作人员的素质和技能要求也随之提高。

本教材是为高职高专学生在完成基础英语的同时,进一步提高其对本专业英语的听说读写能力和实际应用能力而编写的。本教材的重点是使学生掌握一定的专业词汇,能够理解和翻译简单的外文文献资料,能够书写本专业一般的科技论文的英文摘要,能理解本专业进口设备的英文说明书,能够与他人进行简单的专业方面的英语交流,从而为学生在学习、交流、求职以及今后的工作等各方面打下一定的英语基础。

在编写过程中,重点考虑到以下几个方面。首先是职业教育的应用性特征要求教材基于生产实践并具备较强的实用性,以学生就业为导向,以实用、够用为度;其次是专业的发展变化要求教材有一定的前瞻性,比如随着循环流化床锅炉的发展和应用,教材中增加了这方面的内容;另外是高职高专学生的英语基础普遍较差,为了便于学生理解,在每章内容前面都配有中文概述。

本教材由清华大学热能工程系杨海瑞副教授主审。全书按 30 学时考虑,分别包括热工基础理论、锅炉、汽轮机、循环流化床锅炉、热电厂、热工仪表及测量、单元机组运行、环境保护 8 个单元的内容,每章内容前配有中文概要,课文后附有生词表及泛读材料。文章选自各类书刊、科学文献等,参阅了阎维平、李瑞杨等编著的同类教材。

由于时间仓促,编者水平所限,书中难免存在疏漏和不妥之处,恳请广大读者批评、指正。

编　者

2007 年 12 月

Contents

2

Part Ⅰ

Thermodynamics and Heat Transfer

● 中文概要
1. 热力系统的定义及分类
2. 热力参数
3. 热力学第一定律的实质
4. 热力学第二定律的表述
5. 热量传递的基本方式

1.1 Basic Concepts of Thermodynamics

1.1.1 Thermodynamic Systems

Most applications of thermodynamics require that the system and its surroundings be defined. A thermodynamic system is defined as a region in space or quantity of matter bounded by a closed surface. The surroundings include everything external to the system, and the system is separated from the surroundings by the system boundaries. These boundaries can be either movable or fixed, either real or imaginary. A thermodynamic system exchanges matter and energy (heat or work) with surroundings.

Acorrding to the nature of the boundaries, we can classify a thermodynamic system as a closed system, an open system, or an isolated system. When the boundaries of a system are such that the system cannot exchange matter with the surroundings, the system is called to be a closed system (Fig. 1-1(a)). The system, however, may exchange energy in the form of heat or work with the surroundings. The boundaries of a closed system may be rigid or variable, but the mass of a closed system cannot change. Hence, the term control mass sometimes is used for this type of system. When the energy crossing the boundaries of a closed system is zero or substantially so, the system may be treated as an isolated system(Fig. 1-1(b)).

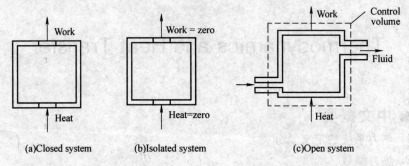

Fig. 1-1 Types of systems

In most engineering problems, matter, generally a fluid, crosses the boundaries of a system in one or more places. Such a system is known as an open system(Fig. 1-1(c)). The boundaries of an open system are so placeable that their location does not change with time. Thus, the boundaries are enclosed by a fixed volume, commonly known as the control volume.

Sometimes a system may be a closed system at one moment and an open one the next. For example, considering the cylinder of an internal combustion engine with the boundaries at the inner walls, with the valves closed, the system is a closed one. However, with either or both of the valves open, the system becomes an open one.

Regardless of a system is a closed system or an open one, if only no (or practically no) heat crosses the boundary, such a system is also defined as an isolated system(adiabatic system).

1. 1. 2　Thermodynamic Properties

A property of a system is any observable characteristic of the system. The state of a system is defined by listing its properties. The most common thermodynamic properties are temperature(T), pressure(P) and specific volume (V) or density (ρ). Additional thermodynamic properties include entropy, stored forms of energy and enthalpy.

Frequently, thermodynamic properties combine to form new properties. Enthalpy(h), a result of combining properties, is defined as:

$$h = U + PV \qquad\qquad (1\text{-}1)$$

where U—internal energy

　　P—pressure

　　V—specific volume

Each property in a given state has only one definite value, and every property always has the same value for a given state, regardless of how the substance arrived at that state.

A process is a change in state that can be defined as any change in the properties of a system. A process is described by specifying the initial and final equilibrium states, the path(if identifiable)and the interactions that take place across the system boundaries during the process. A cycle is a process, or more frequently, a series of processes wherein the initial and final states of the system are identical. Therefore, at the conclusion of a cycle all the properties have the same value they had at the beginning.

Energy is the capacity for producing an effect, and can be categorized into either stored or transient forms. Stored forms of energy include:

Thermal (internal) Energy, U—the energy (possessed by a system) caused by the motion of the molecules and/or intermolecular forces;

Potential Energy, P. E. —the energy (possessed by a system) caused by the attractive forces existing between molecules, or the elevation of the system:

$$\text{P. E.} = mgz \tag{1-2}$$

where m —mass

  g —local acceleration of gravity

  z —elevation above a horizontal reference plane

Kinetic Energy, K. E. —the energy (possessed by a system) caused by the velocity of the molecules:

$$\text{K. E.} = mv^2/2 \tag{1-3}$$

where m —mass

  v —velocity of the fluid streams crossing system boundaries

Chemical Energy, E_c—energy (possessed by the system) caused by the arrangement of atoms composing the molecules.

Nuclear(atomic) Energy, E_a—energy (possessed by the system) from the cohesive forces holding protons and neutrons together as the atom's nucleus.

Transient energy forms include:

Heat, Q—the mechanism(that transfers energy across the boundaries of systems with differing temperatures), always in the direction of the lower temperature.

Work, W—the mechanism that transfers energy across the boundary of systems with differing pressures(or force of any kind), always in the direction of the lower pressure; if the total effect produced in the system can be reduced to the raising of a weight, then nothing but work has crossed the boundary. Mechanical or shaft work, is the energy delivered or absorbed by a mechanism, such as a turbine, air compressor or internal combustion engine.

Flow work is energy carried into or transmitted across the system boundary because a pumping process occurs somewhere outside the system, causing fluid to enter the system. It can be more easily understood as the work done by the fluid just outside the system on the adjacent fluid entering the system to force or push it into the system. Flow work also occurs as fluid leaves the system.

$$\text{Flow work(per unit mass)} = PV \tag{1-4}$$

where P is the pressure and V is the specific volume, or the volume displaced per unit mass.

4

1. 2　The Fundamental Laws of Thermodynamics

1. 2. 1　The First Law of Thermodynamics

Energy can be changed from one form to another, but it cannot be created or destroyed. The total amount of energy and matter in the Universe remains constant, merely changing from one form to another. The First Law of Thermodynamics (Conservation) states that energy is always conserved, it cannot be created or destroyed. In essence, energy can be converted from one form into another.

It is typical for thermodynamics texts to write the first law as equation:

$$Q = \Delta U + W \tag{1-5}$$

where Q—heat added to the system

ΔU—change in internal energy

W—work done on or by the system

It is the general statement of the first law of the thermodynamics, of course—the thermodynamic expression of the conservation of energy principle.

In the context of physics, the common scenario is one of adding heat to a volume of gas and using the expansion of that gas to do work, as in the pushing down of a piston in an internal combustion engine, or as in the steam turbine. In the context of chemical reactions and process, it may be more common to deal with situations where work is done on the system rather than by it.

1. 2. 2　The Second Law of Thermodynamics

The second law of thermodynamics is a general principle which places constraints upon the direction of heat transfer and the attainable efficiencies of heat engines. In so doing, it goes beyond the limitations imposed by the first law of thermodynamics. Its implications may be visualized in terms of the waterfall analogy.

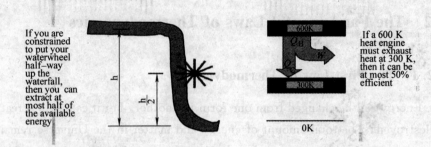

If you are constrained to put your waterwheel half-way up the waterfall, then you can extract at most half of the available energy

If a 600 K heat engine must exhaust heat at 300 K, then it can be at most 50% efficient

The maximum efficiency which can be achieved is the Carnot efficiency.

Second Law of Thermodynamics: It is impossible to extract an amount of heat Q_H from a hot reservoir and use it all to do work W. Some amount of heat Q_C must be exhausted to a cold reservoir. This precludes a perfect heat engine.

This is sometimes called the "first form" of the second law, and is referred to as the Kelvin-Planck statement of the second law.

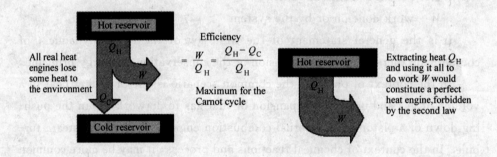

All real heat engines lose some heat to the environment

Efficiency

$$= \frac{W}{Q_H} = \frac{Q_H - Q_C}{Q_H}$$

Maximum for the Carnot cycle

Extracting heat Q_H and using it all to do work W would constitute a perfect heat engine, forbidden by the second law

Second Law of Thermodynamics: It is not possible for heat to flow from a colder body to a warmer body without any work having been done to accomplish this flow. Energy will not flow spontaneously from a low temperature object to a higher temperature object. This precludes a perfect refrigerator. The statements about refrigerators apply to air conditioners and heat pumps, which embody the same principles. This is the "second form" or "Clausius statement" of the second law.

6

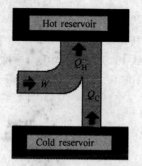

All real refrigerators require work to get heat to flow from a cold area to a warmer area

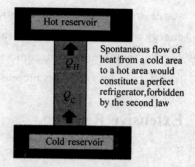

Spontaneous flow of heat from a cold area to a hot area would constitute a perfect refrigerator, forbidden by the second law

1.3 General Characteristics of Heat Transfer

From the study of thermodynamics, you have learned that energy can be transferred by interactions of a system with its surroundings. These interactions are called work and heat. However, thermodynamics deals with the end states of the process during which an interaction occurs and provides no information concerning the nature of the interaction or the time rate at which it occurs. The objective of this section is to extend thermodynamic analysis through study of the modes of heat transfer and through development of relations to calculate heat transfer rates.

What is heat transfer? Heat transfer (or heat) is energy in transit due to a temperature difference. Whenever there exists a temperature difference in a medium or between media, heat transfer must occur.

How is heat transferred? Heat is transferred from one region to another by three modes: conduction, convection and radiation. When a temperature gradient exists in a stationary medium, which may be a solid or a fluid, we use the term conduction to refer to the heat transfer that will occur across the medium. In contrast, the term convection refers to heat transfer that will occur between a surface and a moving fluid when they are at different temperatures. All surface of finite temperature emit energy in the form of electromagnetic waves. Hence, in the absence of an intervening medium, there is net heat transfer by radiation between two surfaces at different temperatures.

In conduction and convection, heat transfer takes place through matter. For radiant heat transfer, there is a change in energy form from internal energy at the source to electromagnetic energy for transmission, then back to internal energy at the receiver. Whereas conduction and convection are affected primarily by temperature difference and somewhat by temperature level, the heat transferred by radiation increases rapidly as the temperature increases.

Extensive Reading

Heat and Work

When hot tea is poured into a cold cup, the tea is cooled and the cup is warmed; a lump of ice cools a glass of lemonade as itself warms and melts. From these and many other everyday examples we learn that heat passes readily from a hot body to a colder one, but not in the opposite direction. This fact is important in the study of thermal energy, and is rather grandly known as the "Second Law of Thermodynamics". This law was announced in about 1850 by two men. One was Lord Kelvin, a famous British scientist. The other discoverer was Rudolph Clausius, a professor of physics in Berlin, and he stated the law thus: "heat cannot of itself (that is without the performance of work by some external agency) pass from a cold to a warmer body". We shall see that it follows from this law that the heat energy in the world is continually becoming less useful to us.

Thermodynamics is the part of science that deals with changes between heat energy and mechanical work. We have already touched on its first law although we did not call it by that name: it is the law that came from the experiments of Joule and others, and it states that: "When work is transformed into heat, or heat into work, the quantity of work is mechanically equivalent to the quantity of heat." This is one particular way of saying that energy is neither gained nor lost, but only changed from one kind to another.

There is another way in which heat energy becomes less useful to us. As Clausius stated the second law of thermodynamics, it says that energy has to be supplied to transfer heat from a cold body to a hot one. Lord Kelvin put the law the other way round by pointing out that heat energy can be used to drive all engine to do mechanical work only by supplying heat to the engine from a high temperature source, and taking it from the engine at a lower temperature. For instance, a steam turbine(Fig. 1-2)may take steam from its boiler at about 900 ℉, and give it up to its exhaust condenser at 212 ℉ , the boiling point water.

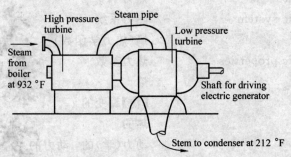

Fig. 1-2 Steam turbine

Steam is supplied by the boiler at a temperature of 932 ℉ , and leaves the exhaust pipe at 212 ℉. The heat energy of the steam is partly converted into mechanical energy which drives all electric generator

New Words and Expressions

thermodynamics *n.*	热力学
thermodynamic system	热力系统
entropy *n.*	熵（热力学函数）
thermodynamic properties	热力参数
enthalpy *n.*	焓
transient *a.*	【物】瞬变的
thermal *a.*	热的
kinetic *a.*	动力（学）的，动力的
cohesive *a.*	内聚的
cohesive forces	内聚力
shaft work	轴功
specific volume	比容
saturation *n.*	饱和（状态）
saturated *a.*	饱和的
flow work *n.*	流动功
equilibrium state	平衡状态
elevation *n.*	高度
acceleration *n.*	加速，加速度
adiabatic process	绝热过程
cyclic process/cycle	循环
categorize *v.*	把……分类
configuration *n.*	构造，结构
quasi-static process	准静态过程
reversible process	可逆过程
closed system	封闭系统
open system	开放系统
isolated system	孤立系统
adiabatic system	绝热系统

Part Ⅱ Boiler

● 中文概要

1. 锅炉的分类及发展趋势
2. 燃料的特点及燃烧过程
3. 煤粉炉的组成设备和工作过程
4. 炉膛、水冷壁的结构特点
5. 过热器、再热器的结构及运行特点
6. 省煤器、空气预热器的结构及运行特点
7. 对流受热面的腐蚀及磨损问题

2.1 Introduction

2.1.1 Types and Classification of Steam Boiler

Boilers use heat to convert water into steam for a variety of applications.

11

Since the time of James Watt, the technology of design and manufacture of steam boilers have been fully developed. Boilers of various designs and different capacities are manufactured for different purposes. Therefore, boilers are classified according to the purpose of their use, to the fuel fired, to the parameters of the steam, to the ways to make steam and water flow in the evaporation heating surfaces, etc.

In China, boilers of steam capacity less than 10 kg/s are called industrial boilers. Those boilers of big capacity supplying steam for turbo-generators in steam power stations are called utility boilers. Boilers are also called by the pressure of the steam generated as following:

4 MPa —medium pressure boiler;

10 MPa —high pressure boiler;

14 MPa —super high pressure boiler;

17~18 MPa —subcritical pressure boiler;

>22.19 MPa —supercritical pressure boiler.

According to the fuels used to fire the boiler, boilers are also called coal fired boiler, oil fired boiler, and gas fired boiler. Furthermore, for coal fired boilers, they are again called by the method of combustion of coal: stoker fired boiler, pulverized-coal fired boiler, and fluidized-bed combustion boiler.

According to the method to keep the water and steam flow in the evaporating heating surface, boilers are called: natural circulation boiler, forced circulation boiler, and once through boiler.

2.1.2 Trend of Development of Technology of Boiler Engineering

2.1.2.1 The Power Pushing Forwards the Development of Boiler Engineering

The era of steam power has existed already more than a century since the beginning of nineteenth century, and has been deliberately developed. So has been the development of boiler engineering indispensable to steam power engineering. Even now, although nuclear power is being developed fast, fossil fuel fired steam power plants are still the main suppliers of power to the world, and is still growing fast, mostly in developing countries.

At first, the main power that pushing forward the development of boiler engineering is the raise of prices and shortage of supply of fuels. In developed countries, coal mines have been mined for one or even two hundred years. Coals from seams far under ground, or coal mines that are hard to mine are now mined. Some mines are now nearly depleted already, coals have to be shipped from far away places. All these raise the price of coals. Petroleum and natural gas reserves of developed countries is not reliable due to political crises. Therefore conservation of energy becomes very important. In China, the annual production of coal since 1990 has become the first in the world, however, the development of economy is faster than the growth of coal production. Therefore, the supply of coal is still insufficient. Besides, the price of coal was abnormally low, and has to be adjusted. Both of these reasons make the price of coal raised significantly. Conservation of coal becomes more and more important. Therefore, to improve boiler efficiencies and to use steam of high parameters are strived for. Besides, the shortage of supply of coals of high quality forces power plants to fire coal of lower quality. All these are pushing forward the development of the technology relevant to steam boiler design.

Secondly, the protection of ecological environment is another initiative that pushes forward the development. the consumption of fuels is increasing, the emission of gaseous and particulate pollutants is increasing, which gives a great impact on ecological environment. Therefore, all the countries are doing something to control the pollution due to coal combustion, to improve the ecological environment. Industries are developing fast in China these years, and the pollution of ecological environment, which is becoming more and more serious, should be curbed effectively. Carbon dioxide, which was considered as harmless, is now considered also as a pollutant that cause green house effect of the globe. Therefore, the quantity of emission of carbon dioxide should also be reduced by more effective use of the heat from fuels.

On the other hand, the development of fundamental science, electronic computer and computer science, is pushing forward the boiler engineering, from relying on empirical design to more theoretical calculation. Thus, the designs of boilers are more and more precise, rational, and reliable, and the performance of new boilers is improved.

2. 1. 2. 2 The Trend of Raise of Steam Parameters and Capacity of Steam Boilers

To raise the pressure and temperature of steam generated from boilers is one of the effective methods to promote the effectiveness of utilization of the heat energy of fuels. For example, a boiler and steam turbine block of 400 MW, the efficiency of power supply will be improved by 1. 4% if the parameters of steam are raised from sub-critical to super-critical pressure. Or in other words, from 36. 4% to 38. 8%, while the initial cost of that block will be increased by 2. 4%. That is still considered as reasonable.

In the United States, the first super-critical boiler started to operate in 1953. In the year of 1957 another super-critical boiler and steam turbine block of 31 MPa, 566/621/638 ℃ was put into operation. Not long after that, several super-critical units were put into operation around 1960. Among these units, the steam parameters of Eddystone Power Station were the highest, 34. 5 MPa, 649/566/566 ℃. However, troubles were confronted in operation, and the parameters were reduced to 31 MPa, 607 ℃ in operation. Nowadays, the technique of super-critical pressure power plant becomes matured, and most of the parameters are around 24. 12 MPa, 538/538 ℃.

The former Soviet Union, developed super-critical units in 1960. In 1963 a 300 MW unit was put into operation. Since then, super-critical units of 500 MW and 800 MW units with boilers of 458 kg/s and 736 kg/s were put into operation. The parameters of steam were 25 MPa, 545/545 ℃.

Japan started to use super-critical pressure boiler since 1967. The parameters of steam were generally 24. 12 MPa, 538/538 ℃, or 538/566 ℃, or 538/552/556 ℃.

Super-critical pressure boilers have already been adopted in power industry in China. The units installed in new power plants at Jixian, Tianjin and Suizhong of Liaoning, and the second power station at Shidongkou, Shanghai are all super-critical pressure ones. The steam parameters of the 600 MW block of Shidongkou are 25 MPa, 541/569 ℃, and the steam output of the boiler is 527. 8 kg/s.

When super-critical pressure units are used, the specific fuel consumption is reduced, and the emission of pollutants is also reduced. That is of course good for environmental protection. Super-critical pressure boiler and turbine are now developed in China.

Co-generation of heat and electric power is also advantageous to improve the effectiveness of utilization of the heat energy of fuels, because in co-generation power plants, the ordinary heat loss to steam condenser is partially or even completely avoided, and utilized as heat supply to industry or heating of homes. Thus, small and inefficient boiler houses for heating can be subsided, great amount of fuels are saved and consequently less pollutants are emitted. Industrial co-generation power plants, and co-generation power plants for domestic heating can save a great amount of fuels and reduce the pollution of environment.

By approximate estimation, if a factory establishes an industrial co-generation power plant of its own instead of using electric power from the net and supplying heat to its work shops by boiler house of low efficiency, 30%～40% of fuel can be saved.

It is clear that, the parameters of steam should be raised to reduce the specific fuel consumption of power supply. Besides, the capacities and parameters of industrial boilers should be raised to meet the requirement of co-generation industrial power plants. As to the capacities of utility boilers, should be raised to 300～600 MW to meet the requirement of power industry.

2. 2 Fuel and Combustion

2. 2. 1 Fuel Classification

The fuels used in most steam generators are coal, natural gas and oil. However, during the past few decades, nuclear energy has also begun to play a major role in at least the electric power generation area. Also, an increasing variety of biomass materials and process byproducts have become heat sources for steam generation. These include peat, wood and wood wasters, bagasse, straw, coffee grounds, corn husks, coal mine wastes (culm), waste heat from steel-making furnaces and even solar energy.

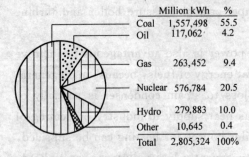

	Million kWh	%
Coal	1,557,498	55.5
Oil	117,062	4.2
Gas	263,452	9.4
Nuclear	576,784	20.5
Hydro	279,883	10.0
Other	10,645	0.4
Total	2,805,324	100%

Fig. 2-1 U. S. net electricity generation by energy source during 1900—23,835. 3 billion kWh

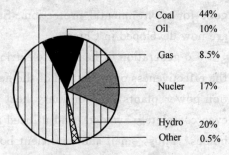

Coal	44%
Oil	10%
Gas	8.5%
Nucler	17%
Hydro	20%
Other	0.5%

Fig. 2-2 Worldwide net electricity generation by energy source during 1988—10,537. 6 billion kWh

The basic types of fuels used for U. S. electricity generation in 1900 are shown in Fig. 2-1. The dominant fuel in modern U. S. central stations is coal, either bituminous, subbituminous or lignite. A similar picture emerges if worldwide electric power production is considered (Fig. 2-2). While natural gas or fuel oil may be the fuel of choice for selected future fossil fuel power plants, coal expected to continue its dominant role in supplying energy to new, base loaded utility power station boilers. With this in mind, the following material focuses primarily on coal-fired utility boiler.

2.2.2 Combustion of Pulverized-coal (PC)

When a coal particle is carried by primary air into the furnace, at first, it is heated by the heat of the flame and the gases in the furnace, the moisture of it is evaporated immediately. Then, its volatile matter starts to come out. If the surrounding temperature is high enough, it is ignited and burns around the coal particle until the volatile matter is depleted, and the coal particles becomes coke particles, consist of fixed carbon and ash. However, these coke particles have already been heated to red hot by the burning of the volatile matter around them. They will continue to burn.

At first, a film of carbon-monoxide will form around the coke particles, the speed of combustion is limited by the speed of the diffusion of the oxygen molecules through the film of CO, while the CO of the film is burning at the outside surface of the film with air, and CO_2 is formed. If the turbulence of the air is high, then the speed of diffusion is also high, the speed of the combustion is controlled by chemical kinetics. The time of residence of a coal particle in a furnace is rather short, one or two seconds, therefore, in the combustion of pulverized-coal, efforts are spent to speed up the combustion, in order that, at the exit of the furnace, the combustion of the coal particle is very close to complete.

As stated above, pulverized coal is carried by furnace through the burners for combustion. However, this part of the air, which is only a small part of the air needed for complete combustion of the coal, is called the primary air. The rest part of the air is called the secondary air, sometimes, even another part of the combustion air is sent into the furnace separately, which is called the tertiary air, or over fire air. The coal particles have to be heated to temperature high enough to get ignited. The primary air has to be heated at the same time. The heat source is the radiation of the flame, and the mixing of the primary air and the coal particles with the high temperature gases in the furnace. If too much air is used as the primary air, the heat needed to heat up the mixture of primary air and pulverized-coal will be higher. The ignition of the coal particles will be harder and slower. Therefore, proper amount of primary air is important to make pulverized-coal ignited as quickly as possible, when they are discharged into the furnace. Of course, for coal with higher volatile matter content, greater amount of primary air can be used, vice versa.

2.3 System Arrangement and Key Components

Modern steam generators are a complex configuration of thermal-hydraulic (steam and water) sections which preheat and evaporate water, and superheat steam. These surfaces are arranged so that: the fuel can be burned completely and efficiently while minimizing emissions; the steam is generated at the required flow rate, pressure and temperature; and the maximum amount of energy is recovered. A relatively simple coal-fired utility boiler is illustrated in Fig. 2-3. The major components in the steam generating and heat recovery system include:

- ◆ Furnace and convection pass
- ◆ Steam superheaters (primary and secondary)
- ◆ Steam reheaters
- ◆ Boiler or steam generating bank(industrial units only)
- ◆ Economizer
- ◆ Steam drum
- ◆ Attemperator and steam temperature control system
- ◆ Air heater

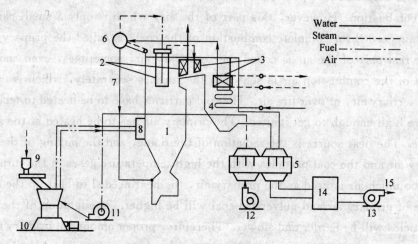

Water ————
Steam – – – – –
Fuel – · – · –
Air – ·· – ·· –

Fig. 2-3   Coal-fired Boiler

1—Furnace; 2—Superheater; 3—Reheater; 4—Economizer; 5—Air heater; 6—Drum; 7—Down comer;
8—Burner; 9—Coal feeder; 10—Pulverizer; 11—Primary air fan; 12—Forced draft fan; 13—Induced draft fan;
14—Precipitators; 15—Exhaust

2.3.1   Furnace

The furnace is a large enclosed open space for fuel combustion and for cooling of the flue gas before it enters the convection pass. Excessive gas temperatures leaving the furnace and entering the tube bundles could cause particle accumulation on the tubes or excessive tube metal temperature. The specific geometry and dimensions of the furnace are highly influenced by the fuel and type of combustion equipment. In this case, finely ground or pulverized coal is blown into the furnace where it burns in suspension. The products of combustion then rise through the upper furnace. The superheater, reheater and economizer surfaces are typically located in the horizontal and vertical downflow sections of the boiler enclosure(convection pass).

In modem steam generators, the furnace and convection pass walls are composed of steam-cooled or water-cooled carbon steel or low alloy tubes to maintain wall metal temperatures within acceptable limits. These tubes are connected at the top and bottom by headers, or manifolds. These headers distribute or collect the water, steam or steam-water mixture. The furnace wall tubes in most modem units also serve as key steam generating components or surfaces. The tubes are welded together with steel bars to provide membrane wall panels which are gas-tight, continuous and rigid. The tubes are usually prefabricated into shippable membrane panels with openings for burners, observation doors, sootblowers (boiler cleaning equipment) and gas injection ports.

2. 3. 2 Superheaters

2. 3. 2. 1 Duty and Types of Superheaters

Superheaters are used to heat the saturated steam from steam drum to become superheated to the specified superheated steam temperature. Besides, the design of the superheater system must be able to maintain the normal specified superheated steam temperature from full load to nearly half load operation of the boiler, or when the moisture of the coal burnt, or the coefficient of excess air, and other conditions of operation are changed.

Inside the superheater tubes, steam of high pressure flows, or in other words, the superheater tubes are subjected to high pressure. Besides, to get higher temperature difference to intensify the heat transfer, superheaters are installed where the flue gas temperature is high. Sometimes, they receive the intensive heat radiation from the flame directly. The tube wall temperature of superheaters are generally high, therefore, they are made mostly of alloy steel to withstand the high temperature and high pressure.

Superheaters can be classified as convective and radiant ones, or sometimes, semi-radiant superheaters. The characteristics of convective superheater is that, the superheated steam temperature lowers as the boiler load decreases. Contrarily, the superheated steam temperature of radiant superheater rises as the boiler load decreases. If the superheater of a boiler is designed partially convective, in some occasion, the superheated steam temperature may remain constant at load variation. However, that would be difficult, because the portion of the heat absorption of the radiant superheater should be greater than that of the convective one, that is hard to realize in practice.

In most cases, the superheater system, which consists of several sections, is designed to absorb heat more than enough at full load, the excessive heat is absorbed by water spray in a desuperheater, by regulating the amount of water spray, the superheated steam temperature is kept constant at the specified value during load variation. Of course, at low load, the amount of water spray is reduced.

2.3.2.2 Design of Superheater

In superheater design, the following problems should be considered carefully to make it more reliable in operation and less expensive in manufacture:

(1) Use combination of radiant and convective superheater sections;

(2) Proper arrangement of one or two spray desuperheaters;

(3) Use correct connections and form a superheater section;

(4) Use cross and mixing connections;

(5) Use proper mark of carbon or alloyed steel according to the working temperature of the tube wall;

(6) High enough steam flow velocity in tubes;

(7) Final stage of regulation of steam temperature by desuperheater should be installed at the inlet of the final superheater of relatively lower heat absorption, thus the time lag will be shorter.

If the points mentioned above are considered properly, the superheater designed will be reliable in operation, low in cost, and have better temperature characteristics.

2.3.3 Reheater

Reheaters are used in high pressure steam cycles to improve the thermal efficiency. Generally, the steam temperature of reheat steam is as high as the primary superheated steam. However, the regulation of reheat steam temperature is much more difficult than the primary superheated steam, because at low load, the temperature of income reheat steam is reduced significantly, thus the requirement of regulation is more serious. Besides, during starting up or sudden shutting down of the boiler, there will be no reheat steam flow through the reheater, therefore, the heating surface of reheater has to be protected with special care. Radiant reheater is not practical in the consideration of protection during starting up and shutting down.

Water spray should not be used in the regulation of reheat steam temperature, because that would decrease the thermal efficiency of the power plant significantly. Since the water sprayed into reheat steam is evaporated at medium pressure, which implies that, the high pressure cycle is working in combination with a small medium pressure cycle with lower thermal efficiency. Therefore, the more water sprayed, the more the decrease of thermal efficiency of the power plant. Therefore, water spray is not used in normal regulation of reheat steam temperature, but is used only as a measure of protection of reheater during accidents.

Generally reheater is composed of two tube banks, one behind the high temperature superheater, the other before the economizer. The regulation of the steam temperature is mostly realized by damper control. The pressure drop of reheat steam should be kept as low as possible to make its influence on thermal efficiency to minimum. Therefore, greater tube diameter and lower steam flow velocity are used in reheater design. Tube diameter of $\Phi42\times3.5$ or $\Phi44.5\times3.5$ is used in reheaters.

2.3.4 Economizer

The economizer is a counterflow heat exchanger for recovering energy from the flue gas beyond the superheater and, if used, the reheater. It increases the temperature of the water entering the steam drum. The tube bundle is typically an arrangement of parallel horizontal serpentine tubes with the water flowing inside but in the opposite direction(counterflow)to the flue gas. Tube spacing is as tight as possible to promote heat transfer while still permitting adequate tube surface cleaning and limiting flue gas side pressure loss. By design, steam is usually not generated inside these tubes.

The most common and reliable economizer design is the bare tube, in-line,

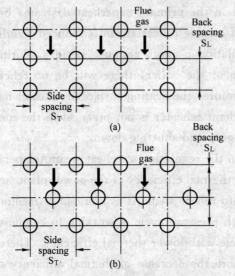

Fig. 2-4 Bare tube economizer arrangement

crossflow type(Fig. 2-4(a)). When coal is fired, the fly ash creates a high foul and erosive environment. The bare tube, in-line arrangement minimizes the likelihood of erosion and trapping the ash as compared to a staggered arrangement shown in Fig. 2-4(b). It is also the easiest geometry to be kept clean by sootblowers. However, these benefits must be evaluated against the possible larger weight, volume and cost of this arrangement.

To reduce capital costs, most boiler manufactures have built economizers with a variety of fin types to enhance the controlling gas side heat transfer rate. Fins are inexpensive nonpressure parts which can reduce the overall size and cost of an economizer. However, successful application is very sensitive to the flue gas environment. Surface cleanability is a key concern.

Stud fins have worked reasonably well in gas-fired boiler, but studded fins have performed poorly in coal-fired boilers because of high erosion, loss of heat transfer, increased pressure loss and plugging resulting from fly ash deposits.

Longitudinally-finned tubes in staggered crossflow arrangements have also performed well over long operating periods. Excessive plugging and erosion in coal-fired boilers have resulted in the replacement of many of these economizers.

Helically-finned tubes have been successfully applied to some coal-fired, oil-fired and gas-fired units. If heavy fuel oil or coal is fired, a wider fin spacing must be used and adequate measures taken to keep the heating surface as clean as possible.

The square or rectangular fins, arranged perpendicular to the tube axis on in-line tubes have had some success in retrofits.

The tube ends should be fully baffled to minimize flue gas bypass in finned bundles. Such bypass flow can reduce heat transfer, produce excessive casing temperatures and with coal firing, can lead to tube bend erosion because of very high gas velocities. Baffling is also used with bare tube bundles but is not as important as for finned tube bundles.

Higher velocities provide better heat transfer and reduce capital cost. For clean burning fuels, such as gas and low ash oil, velocities are typically set by the maximum economical pressure loss. For high ash oil and coal, gas side velocities are limited by the erosion potential of the fly ash. This erosion potential is primarily determined by the percentage of Al_2O_3 and SiO_2 in the ash, the total ash in the fuel and the gas maximum velocity.

For a given tube arrangement and boiler load, the gas velocity depends on the specific volume of flue gas which falls as the flue gas is cooled in the economizer. To maintain the gas velocity, it can be economical to decrease the free flow gas side cross section by selecting a larger tube size in the lower bank of a multiple bank design. This achieves better heat transfer and reduces the total heating surface.

Water in economizer should flow upward to facilitate the carrying away of dissolved air bubbles when heated to avoid water side corrosion of the tube. When no evaporation takes place in the economizer, i. e. , in non-boiling economizer, the average flow velocity of water should be higher than 0. 3 m/s. For boiling economizer, the average flow velocity of water should be higher than 1 m/s. The fraction of steam at the outlet of a boiling economizer should not exceed 25%, otherwise, the pressure drop of the economizer will be too high. Literally, the pressure drop should not exceed 8% of the pressure of the steam drum. The flow velocity of flue gas in economizer tube bank is generally $1\sim13$ m/s. For coal of high ash content the lower value of gas velocity should be used.

2.3.5 Air Preheater

Economizers recover the energy by heating the boiler feedwater while air heaters heat the combustion air. The air heater utilizes the heat in the boiler flue gases leaving the economizer to heat the combustion air and provide hot air for drying coal. An improvement of 1% in boiler efficiency is achieved for 22 °C rise in the coal combustion air temperature. The air outlet temperature limit in coal fired plant is dictated by the coal mill exit temperature and capacity of the tempering air system with the gas outlet temperature limited by considerations of fouling of the heat transfer surface and corrosion of downstream equipment. Air heating also enhances the combustion of many fuels and ensuring stable ignition.

In utility boilers either tubular or rotary air preheaters are used. For boilers of capacity higher than 200 MW, the arrangement of tubular air preheater becomes difficult. It can hardly be arranged in the vertical convective shaft of the boiler, besides, too much steel will be used. In such case, rotary air preheater is used instead.

In tubular air preheater, tubes of $\Phi 40 \times 1.5$ are used. Flue gas flows inside the tubes while air flows outside cross the tubes. The tubes are in staggered arrangement, with transverse pitch of $60 \sim 70$ mm and longitudinal pitch of 50 mm. The gas velocity in the tubes is generally around $10 \sim 14$ m/s, the air velocity across the tube bank is $45\% \sim 55\%$ of the gas velocity. When the required temperature of preheated air is relatively high, air has to flow in several paths of the air preheater, as shown in Fig. 2-5.

The lowest part of the air preheater where cold air enters it is subjected to corrosion due to possible condensation of water vapor in the flue gas, because the tube wall at that place might be lower than the dew point of the flue gas. To facilitate change of tubes of that part of heating surface, this part of the air preheater is made as an independent tube section. For boilers of larger capacity, it is hard to make the air velocity low enough. To solve this problem, air is supplied to air preheater from both front and rear sides of the air preheater, as shown in Fig. 2-6.

Rotary, or so called Ljunstrom air preheaters are frequently used both in smaller or large capacity boilers. A rotor of great diameter is installed in the air preheater housing. Inside the rotor, the space is divided into sections, in which corrugated steel sheet heating surfaces of thickness of 0.5 mm are installed. The rotor is driven by a motor to rotate from 0.75 to 2.5 rpm. The vertical shaft of the rotor is supported by two bearings one above, and one beneath the rotor.

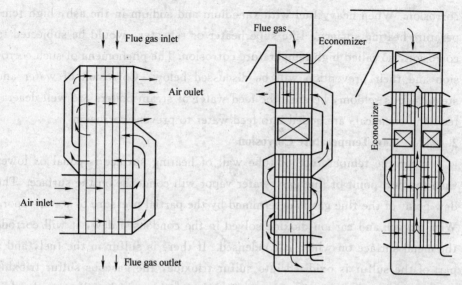

Fig. 2-5　Flow passage of air in air preheater

Fig. 2-6　Arrangement of air preheater in boilers of medium and large capacity

Through one half of the rotor (180 ℃), flue gas flows downward, through the other part of the rotor(120 ℃), air flows upward. The rest two sectors of 30 ℃ are the transition zone of the rotor. The heating surfaces in the rotor is heated by flue gas in operation, and heat is accumulated in them. When it rotates to the section where the air flow through, they give heat to the air. Thus the flue gas is cooled down and air is heated. Of course, seals should be provided between the gaps of the ducts for flue gas and air with the rotor to eliminate excessive infiltration of air into flue gas. Seals should also be provided for the gaps between the rotor and the air preheater housing.

2.4　Corrosion and Erosion of Convective Heating Surface and Its Prevention

2.4.1　Corrosion of Convective Heating Surfaces and Its Prevention

When coal of high moisture and high sulfur content is burnt, low temperature heating surfaces would be subjected to corrosion, so called low temperature corrosion. When heavy fuel with vanadium and sodium in the ash, high temperature heating surface, like superheater or reheater, would be subjected to corrosion, so called high temperature corrosion. The phenomena of such corrosion and their prevention will be discussed below. Corrosion of water and steam side is seldom, because the feed water of steam boilers are well deaerated, and chemicals are added into feed water to prevent corrosion.

2. 4. 1. 1 Low Temperature Corrosion

When the temperature of tube wall of heating surface is equal or lower than the dew point of flue gas, water vapor will condense on the surface. The dew point of the flue gas is determined by the partial pressure of water vapor. With oxygen and carbon dioxide solved in the condensed dew, it will corrode the metal surface on which it condensed. If there is sulfur in the fuel, and a part of the sulfur is oxidized into sulfur trioxide, the gaseous sulfur trioxide will combine with water into vapor of sulfuric acid, which will raise the dew point of the flue gas greatly. The problem of corrosion will be more serious.

Generally, the dew point of water vapor in flue gas is quite low, condensation would not likely happen on heating surfaces. With the presence of sulfur trioxide, the dew point is raised greatly. In Table 2-1 the dew point of pure water vapor with respect to its partial pressure, and the dew point with presence of sulfur trioxide are listed. The effect of the partial pressure of SO_3 is clearly shown. The dew point with presence of sulfuric acid vapor is called acid dew point.

Table 2-1   Dew Point of Flue Gas with Sulfuric Acid in Presence

Partial pres. of H_2SO_4 (Pa)	Partial pres. of water vapor (Pa)		
	5,000	8,300	24,500
0	33	43	64
10	40	48	70
50	63	68	87
100	86	91	105
200	116	121	130

With the theory of physicochemistry, the concentration of sulfuric acid in the condensed dew will be rather high, when the heating surface equals or is lower than the acid dew point. The sulfuric acid condensation of mixture of water vapor and sulfuric acid vapor is shown in Fig. 2-7. Therefore, the corrosion could be rather strong. However, the corrosion of concentrated sulfuric acid is not as strong as sulfuric acid of medium concentration. When the flue gas flowing to heating surface of lower temperature down stream, it loses some of its sulfuric acid due to previous condensation, therefore, the concentration of sulfuric acid condensed is decreasing. The effect of corrosion is also changing as the example shown in Fig. 2-8. During load variation, the zone of strong corrosion will move along the heating surface.

To prevent excessive corrosion of low temperature heating surface, the following measures are used.

(1) Warm up the air before it enters the air preheater in a forewarmer by bled steam from the steam turbine.

(2) Reduce the formation of sulfur trioxide in the combustion by using low excess air.

(3) Use corrosion resistant materials, such as ceramic or glass as the heating surface of air preheater.

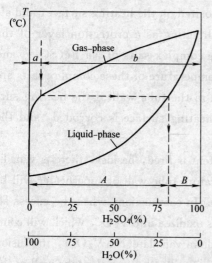

Fig. 2-7 Concentration of sulfuric acid in condensation of mixture of water vapor and sulfur acid vapor

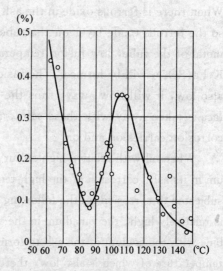

Fig. 2-8 Speed of corrosion with respect to tube wall temperature

(4) Use the construction of air preheater with air flows in the tubes and flue gas flows across the tube bank, thus the wall temperature is closer to the flue gas temperature.

2.4.1.2 High Temperature Corrosion

High temperature corrosion may happen both in coal and oil fired boilers. When coal with both alkaline and sulfur in its ash, corrosion of high temperature heating surface may be subjected to high temperature corrosion, while fuel oil is fired, when there is vanadium in the ash and sulfur content is relatively high. the high temperature heating surface may also be subjected to high temperature corrosion.

When coal of high alkaline content in its ash, in the combustion, the sodium and potassium in the ash is oxidized into sodium oxide(Na_2O) and potassium oxide(K_2O), which sublimate in the furnace at high temperature, and then they condense on tube wall of high temperature convective heating surface, mostly the superheater. When a part of the sulfur in coal is oxidized into sulfur trioxide, it will combine with the condensed oxides of alkaline, form salts, sodium and potassium sulfate. The fusion temperature of these salts is low. When there is ferrous oxide in the ash deposited on the heating surface, and also the ferrous oxide layer on the tube wall acting as a protection layer of the metal of the tube, low fusion temperature complex salts of $Na_3Fe(SO_4)_3$ and $K_3Fe(SO_4)_3$ will be formed. The fusion temperature of these complex salts are also low, it will flow away, thus the iron in the tube wall of the heating surface is taken away with these salts, the heating surface is corroded, and the corrosion carries on and on.

When oil with relative high sulfur content is fired, besides, there is vanadium in its ash, corrosion of the high temperature tube wall of superheater will be subjected to corrosion by the following way. In combustion, when the excess air is relatively high, the vanadium in the ash is oxidized into V_2O_5, which will combine with the sodium in the ash to form sodium vanadate($Na_4V_2O_7$), the fusion temperature of which is also low, therefore, it will adhere on the tube wall of the high temperature superheater. If the temperature of the tube wall is over 600 ℃, the liquid sodium vanadate will transport oxygen to the tube wall and oxidize the tube wall. This is one of the explanations of the phenomenon of high temperature corrosion, there are also other explanations.

It was found that, if the tube wall temperature is lower than 580 ℃, the speed of high temperature corrosion will be reduced to a tolerable value. Therefore, to prevent high temperature corrosion lower superheated steam temperature is used. On the other hand, low excess air is used in combustion, thus less sulfur trioxide is formed. In modern utility boilers, superheated steam and reheated steam temperature of 538~540 ℃ is used, and for oil firing, only 3% of excess air is used in the combustion to avoid high temperature corrosion.

2.4.2　Erosion of Convective Heating Surfaces

When pulverized-coal is fired, more than 90% of its ash is entrained by flue gas. The erosion caused by these ash particles is inevitable. However, by correct consideration in design, the speed of erosion can be reduced to tolerable speed.

The speed of erosion is in direct proportion to the amount of ash particle passing through the tube bank per unit cross-section in unit time, that is in direct proportion to the velocity of flue gas. Besides, at the same time, the speed of erosion is in direct proportion to the kinetic energy of the ash particles, which is in direct proportion to the square of flue gas velocity. Therefore, the speed of erosion is in direct proportion to the cubic of the velocity of flue gas. Of course, the density and abrasive of the ash particles are also in relation with the speed of erosion. Their influences are taken into account in the proportion constant.

When the flow of flue gas changes its direction, the entrained ash particle will be concentrated by the inertia force to the outside of the turning point. That will make the erosion of this part of heating surface much more serious. If there are short circuit passages in the tube bank, the flow velocity will accelerate in these passages, and the erosion of the heating surface along these passages will be more intensive.

Staggered tube bank will be subjected to much serious erosion than in-line one, because in staggered tube bank, the ash particles pass through the first row of tubes, will be concentrated to impact the second row tubes. This effect of concentration will be the same to the rows behind. While in in-line tube bank, the tubes of the first row will protect the tubes of the rows behind them.

To prevent excess erosion, reasonable flow velocity of flue gas should be chosen, eliminate short circuit passages if possible, shield the tube of the first row of the tube bank and the tube bends adjacent to the walls of the flue. When coal of high ash content is used, tower type layout of the boiler should be used, thus the change of flow direction can be avoided. The reasonable flow velocities of flue gas with respect to the ash content per MJ of heating value are listed in Table 2-2.

Table 2-2 Marginal Gas Velocity of Flue Gas of Pulverized-coal Fired Boilers

Heating Surface	Marginal flow velocity(m/s)				No ash low velocity (m/s)
	Ash content per MJ(g/MJ)				
	<12	14~17	21~24	70	
Economizer	13	10	9	7	8~11
Superheater(Carbon steel)	14	12	11	8	10~14
Superheater(Alloyed steel)					15~20

Extensive Reading

Spiral and Vertical Furnace Circuitry

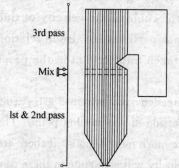

3rd pass

Mix

1st & 2nd pass

Fig. 2-9 Multiple pass vertical tube once-through supercritical pressure boiler furnace circuitry

Base-loaded supercritical pressure once-through boilers operating in the United States have been designed for constant pressure operation. Vertical tubes have been arranged in multiple furnace passes to maintain high mass fluxes for adequate cooling (Fig. 2-9). The fluid is always a single phase because the boilers operate at a constant supercritical pressure and steam-water phase separation is avoided. Intermediate fluid mixing headers have been used to minimize significant variations in the furnace panel outlet steam enthalpy and temperature due to variations in heat input around the boiler perimeter. Large variations could lead to boiler tube and header failures. The furnace water walls are self-supporting using the longitudinal load carrying capability of the vertical tubes.

However, advanced systems can potentially take advantage of one of two other furnace water wall circuitry designs. The first is the spiral circuitry furnace (Fig. 2-10). The vertical multiple-pass system is replaced by inclined tubes which spiral around the furnace enclosure, typically making at least a single pass around the full furnace from the hopper to the upper furnace region where a transition is made to vertical tubes. The circuity is simple with no intermediate mix headers and only a single upward pass through the furnace. High mass fluxes are maintained because the

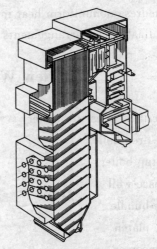

Fig. 2-10 Spiral circuitry furnace

tube orientation reduces the number of tubes required. Each tube receives nearly the same total heat input because each tube passes through all of the heat flux zones in the boiler thus minimizing variations in outlet enthalpy and temperature. This design is also capable of full sliding pressure operation including subcritical pressures — the absence of mixing headers avoids the problems associated with steam water flow separation. Spiral circuitry furnaces, however, do have drawbacks. The furnace walls are not self-supporting because the tubes are inclined, and an external support strap system is needed. The complexity of fabricating the spiral circuitry tube panels in the shop, installing the panels in the field and requiring a support strap system all tend to lead to higher capital costs.

An alternate design which is currently under development for use in sliding pressure boilers is a once-through, once-up vertical tube furnace. In this design, the fluid effectively makes a single pass through the vertical furnace water wall tubes. Complexity and capital cost are reduced because: multiple furnace circuit passes are not used the intermediate fluid mix headers are eliminated and the tubes are vertical and thus self-supporting. Adequate furnace water wall cooling is a key technical issue, especially at low loads where the water or steam flow rate is low. Other issues being evaluated include: flow stability when the unit is operating in the subcritical pressure range, methods to address nonuniform heat input between tubes around the furnace perimeter and final circuit arrangements.

New Words and Expressions

subcritical pressure boiler	亚临界压力锅炉
coal-fired boiler	燃煤锅炉
startup boiler	启动锅炉
furnace wall	炉墙
tube bundle	管束(排)
tube platen	管屏
downcomer n.	下降管
riser n.	上升管
economizer n.	省煤器
reheater n.	再热器
superheated tube	过热器管
coil n.	蛇形管
supporting tube	吊挂管
water wall tube	水冷壁管
saturated steam	饱和蒸汽
boiler proper	锅炉本体
finned tube	鳍片管
header n.	联箱
boiler unit	锅炉机组
boiler framework	燃烧器
furnace n.	炉膛
combustion chamber	燃烧室
damper n.	风门
tube plate	管板
superheater	过热器

soot blower	吹灰器
wall enclosure superheater	包墙过热器
furnace volume	炉膛容积
primary reheater	再热器冷段
steam/moisture separator	汽水分离器
final reheater	再热器热段
air preheater	空气预热器
explosion vent	防爆门
inspection hole	检查孔
three-way valve	三通阀
emergency water spray valve	事故喷水阀
blowdown *n.*	锅炉排污
ash hopper	灰斗
air compressor	空气压缩机
coal pulverizer/coal mill	磨煤机
primary air fan	一次风机
forced draft/forced fan	送风机
induced draft/induced fan	引风机
precipitator *n.*	除尘器
ash pump/slag pump	灰渣泵
air piping	风管道
hydraulic test	水压试验
negative pressure	负压
ignition *n.*	点火
positive pressure	正压
firing point/ignition temperature	着火点

Part Ⅲ

Circulating Fluidized Bed (CFB) Boiler

●中文概要

1. 循环流化床锅炉的工作原理与优点(与煤粉炉比较)
2. 循环流化床锅炉的工作流程与主体结构
3. 分离器种类及结构特点
4. 返料器种类及结构特点

3.1 CFB Technology

3.1.1 Introduction

In Asia, demand for electric power continues to rise steeply due to population growth, economic development, and progressive substitution of alternate technology with lean forms of energy generation. Atmospheric circulating fluidized bed (CFB) technology has emerged as an environmentally acceptable technology for burning a wide range of solid fuels to generate steam and electricity power. CFB, although less than 20 years old, is a mature technology with more than 400 CFB boilers in operation worldwide, ranging from 5 MW to 250 MW.

Electric utilities and independent power producers must now select a technology that will utilize a wide range of low-cost solid fuels, reduce emissions, reduce life cycle costs, and provide reliable steam generation for electric power generation.

Therefore, a circulating fluidized bed is a relatively new and evolving technology that has become a very efficient method of generating low-cost electricity while generating electricity with very low emissions and environmental impacts. Even though pulverized-coal(PC)fired boilers continue to play a major role worldwide, they have inherent issues such as fuel inflexibility, environmental concerns and higher maintenance costs.

3.1.2　What is CFB Technology

CFB technology utilizes the fluidized bed principle in which crushed(6～12 mm × 0 size)fuel and limestone are injected into the furnace or combustor. The particles are suspended in a stream of upwardly flowing air(60%～70% of the total air)which enters the bottom of the furnace through air distribution nozzles. The balance of combustion air is admitted above the bottom of the furnace as secondary air. While combustion takes place at 840～900 ℃, the fine particles(<450 microns)are elutriated out of the furnace with flue gas velocity of 4～6 m/s. The particles are then collected by the solids separators and circulated back into the furnace. This combustion process is called circulating fluidized bed(CFB). The particles' circulation provides efficient heat transfer to the furnace walls and longer residence time for carbon and limestone utilization. Similar to PC firing, the controlling parameters in the CFB combustion process are temperature, residence time and turbulence.

3.1.3　The Comparison of PC and CFB Technology

Designers and power plant operators have vast experience in PC-fired boiler design and operations. Adapting and understanding CFB technology by those familiar with the PC environment requires time. CFB technology brings the capability of designs for a wide range of fuels from low quality to high, lower emissions, elimination of high maintenance pulverizers, low auxiliary fuel support and reduced life cycle costs. The comparison of PC and IR - CFB is given in Table 3-1.

Table 3-1　Benefits of a CFB Boiler over a PC-Fired Boiler(<150 MW)

Description	CFB Boiler	PC-Fired Boiler	Benefits of CFB
Fuel size	6~12 mm×0	>70%, <75 microns	Crushing cost is reduced
Fuel range (ash&moisture)	Up to 75%	Up to 60%	Accepts wider range
Higher sulfur fuels (1%~6%)	Limestone injection	FGD plant required	Less expensive SO_2 removal system
Auxiliary fuel support (oil or gas)	Up to 20%~30%	Up to 60%	Less oil/gas consumption
Auxiliary power consumption	Slightly higher	Lower	If FGD is used in PC, CFB power is lower Emissions
SO_2(ppm)	<200	250	With FGD lower emissions in process, less expensive
NO_x(ppm)	<100	<100	With SCR(or SNCR)system required
Boiler efficiency(%)	Same	Same	No difference
O&M cost(85% CF)	5%~10% lower	5%~10% higher	Lower because of less moving equipment
Capital cost	5%~10% higher　8%~15% lower	5%~10% lower w/o FGD & SCR　8%~15% higher w/o FGD & SCR	—

The combustion temperature of CFB(840~900 ℃)is much lower than PC (1,350~1,500 ℃)which results in lower NO_x(Nitrogen Oxides)formation and the ability to capture SO_2 with limestone injection in the furnace. Even though the combustion temperature of CFB is low, the fuel residence time is higher than PC, which results in good combustion efficiencies comparable to PC. The PC pulverizers, which grind the coal less than 75 microns, require significant maintenance expenses. These costs are virtually eliminated in CFB, because the coal is crushed to 6~12 mm ×0 size. Even though CFB boiler equipment is designed for relatively low flue gas velocities, the heat transfer coefficient of the CFB furnace is nearly double that of PC which makes the furnace compact. In an IR-CFB, auxiliary fuel support is needed for cold startup and operation below 25% versus 40%~60% MCR with PC. One of the most important aspects is that CFB boilers release very low levels of SO_2 and NO_x pollutants compared to PC, as shown in Table 3-1. PC units need a scrubber system, which requires additional maintenance.

3. 2　Characteristics of CFB

3. 2. 1　CFB Is a Fuel-driven and Flexible Technology

CFB can be the technology of choice for several reasons. The CFB can handle a wide range of fuels such as coal, waste coal, anthracite, lignite, petroleum coke and agricultural waste, with low heating value(over 1,500 kcal/kg), high moisture content($< 55\%$), and high ash content(less than 60%). The fuel flexibility provides use of opportunity fuels where uncertainty of fuel supply exists and economics are an issue. If a CFB boiler is designed for coal, the same boiler can be used to burn lignite or petroleum coke or anthracite. The material handling and feeding system should be properly designed to meet these fuel variations. Such fuel flexibility is not available in the competing conventional PC-fired boiler technologies. This is one of the important features of CFB that the customer needs to analyze carefully before selecting a technology.

3. 2. 2　Environmental Benefits of CFB Technology

The CFB combustion process facilitates steam generation firing a wide range of fuels while meeting the required emissions such as sulfur dioxide (SO_2) and nitrogen oxides(NO_x) even more effectively than World Bank requirements, as shown in Table 3-2. The major environmental benefit of selecting CFB technology is the removal of SO_2 ($90\% \sim 95\%$) and NO_x (emission is less than 100 ppm)in the combustion process without adding postcombustion cleaning equipment such as wet or dry flue gas desulfurization(FGD) systems and selective catalytic reduction(SCR) systems.

Table 3-2　CFB Boiler Emissions Compared to the World Bank Emission Requirements

Description	World Bank Emission Requirements	CFB Boiler Emissions
Sulfur dioxide(SO_2)(ppm)	730	<200
Nitrogen oxides(NO_x)(ppm)	365 *	<100
Particulate matter(mg/Nm³)	50+	50

* Coal with 10% volatile matter, NO_x is 730 ppm　　　+ Less than 50 MW, P. M. is 100 mg/Nm³

3.2.3 Advantages

Even though a number of competing technologies are available in the market for steam and electric power generation, CFB is an excellent choice due to its fuel flexibility, wider turndown without supporting oil/gas, superior environmental performance, lower operating and maintenance costs, and safe, reliable and simple boiler operation.

A commercial CFB boiler consists of advantages as following:

(1) burning efficiency reaches 95% ~ 99%;

(2) high burning rate, heat efficiency above 87%;

(3) energy-saving, high efficiency;

(4) high flexibility of fuel, which can satisfy the burning of many kinds of fuels;

(5) limestone can be added in bed material;

(6) during burning process racts with SO_2 of flue formulates sulphate, desurphuration can satisfy environment protection;

(7) reasonable air distribution and low temperature of furnace which can control formulation of NO_x and really reach environment protection;

(8) big adjusting range load can be adjusted ranging from 10% to 30%;

(9) high automatic control, makes boilers running safely and economically in long term;

(10) adopt upper-exhaust high temperature cyclone separated device;

(11) high collection of bed material;

(12) high heat transfer coefficient, high ability of overload.

3.3 Main Body Construction and Key Components

3.3.1 Boiler Configuration

The CFB boiler design consists of the following major systems, shown in Fig. 3-1. The main CFB boiler components are:

◆Boiler furnace

- ◆Furnace bottom air distributor and nozzles
- ◆Primary solids separators and recirculation system
- ◆Secondary solids separators and recirculation system
- ◆Pendant superheater/reheater
- ◆Economizer and horizontal tubular air heater
- ◆Air assisted gravity fuel/limestone feed system

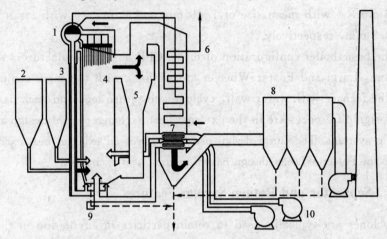

Fig. 3-1　CFB boiler schematic of Ahlstrom Pyroflow

1—Steam drum　2—Fuel　3—Limestone　4—Combustion chamber　5—Hot cyclone
6—Superheaters　7—Air heater　8—Baghouse　9—Ash cooler　10—Secondary air fan

These consist of a combustion chamber, a cyclone separator, a return leg and loop seal or L-valve for recirculation of the bed particles (Tang and Engstrom, 1987). The combustion chamber is enclosed with water-cooled tubes and a gas-tight membrane. The lower section of the combustor is covered with refractory, with openings for introducing fuel, limestone, secondary air, recycled ash, one or more gas or oil burners for startup and bottom ash drains. Most of the combustion occurs in the lower section while heat transfer to the furnace wall is achieved mainly by particle convection and radiation in the upper section of the combustor. The cyclone is refractory-lined and is designed to separate the entrained solids from the hot flue gas and return them through the return leg and loop seal. The loop seal prevents backflow of gas from the riser up the standpipe and has no movable mechanical parts. The gas velocity employed in CFB is usually in the range from 4.5 to 6 m/s. Air is fed to the unit as primary air. Secondary air, transport air for fuel and limestone feed air to the loop seal and fluidizing air to the ash classifier. The bottom ash classifier is designed to remove larger bed particles and recycle small particles back to the combustor for improved heat transfer. The operating bed temperature is usually in the range of 850~900 ℃. This temperature range is chosen to optimize the sulfur capture efficiency of limestone. The coal and limestone feed sizes are typically 6 mm×0 with mean size of 1~3 mm and 1 mm×0 with mean size of 0.1~0.3 mm, respectively.

The basic boiler configuration of major CFB boiler manufacturers such as Ahlstrom, Lurgi and Foster Wheeler are similar, with the main components being the furnace with water wall, cyclone and return leg, and back pass. The main design differences are in the external heat exchanger, grid design and ash handling systems. The Lurgi design usually features an external heat exchanger, whereas the Foster Wheeler design has an internal heat exchanger.

3.3.2 Separator and Return System Features

Cyclones are typically used to retain particles in circulation in the CFB combustor. These can be water-cooled, steam-cooled or without cooling. In other CFB designs, various kinds of impact separators are used such as U-beam and louver-type separators. However, the efficiency of these separators varies. The efficiency of the particle separator affects the combustion efficiency and limestone utilization. The particle separator separates entrained particles from the flue gas stream and returns the particles to the combustor. Hence, the solids mean residence time in the combustor is increased by improving the cyclone efficiency. The recycle system (L-valve or J-valve) works on the principle of pressure balance between the solid return leg and the furnace pressure above the solid recycle point.

Studies have shown that the exit configuration of the combustor has an effect on the internal solids circulation in the combustor. For an abrupt exit, a higher percentage of solids reaching the cyclone fall back to the combustor than for a smooth exit. Typically, commercial CFB units have abrupt exits to the cyclone, which facilitates internal solids recirculation leading to longer solids residence times. An extended top section may increase the internal solids recircula-

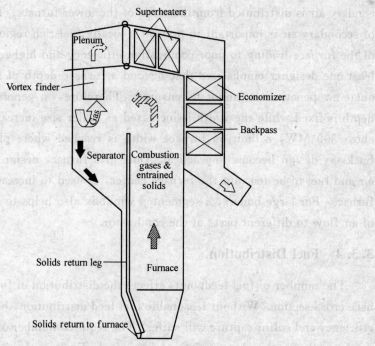

Fig. 3-2 Pyroflow compact concept

tion although cyclones have performed well in CFB units. they have been high cost items. In the development of second generation CFB boilers, designers have tried to replace the cyclone. Substitute candidates for high temperature operation can be divided into three main categories, which include separators built inside the furnace. Traditional high temperature cyclones made of water/ steam-cooled membrane walls and various kinds of particle settling chambers and impact labyrinths designed to collect solids without the use of centrifugal force. For one designer, a new kind of centrifugal separator consisting of fiat walls has been developed to replace the traditional cyclone. This square separation chamber is equipped with a vortex finder and has a collection hopper underneath, which provides for solids return to the lower combustor. Fig. 3-2 shows the new Pyroflow compact design.

3.3.3 Air Distribution

Furnace depth affects air distribution over the furnace cross-section. Secondary air is distributed from the walls of the lower furnace. The penetration of secondary air is important to prevent a locally fuel-rich region at the center of the furnace leading to poor combustion efficiency and higher emissions. At least one designer emphasizes that beyond a furnace depth of $9 \sim 11$ m, adequate air penetration cannot be ensured. Therefore, in general, the furnace depth is fixed while the width is increased as boiler size increases. However, above 300 MW, a limit on furnace width is reached where plant layout and buckstay design become impractical. Dual grid furnace design, which allows air and fuel to be fed into the furnace center, is used to increase the depth of furnace. For large boilers, a segmented windbox also helps to provide control of air flow to different parts of the combustor.

3. 3. 4　Fuel Distribution

The number of fuel feedpoints affects the distribution of fuel over the furnace cross-section. Without reasonable fuel feed distribution, both combustion efficiency and sulfur capture will suffer. The required number of feedpoints depends partly on the characteristics of the fuel. Fuels with high volatile content, such as sub-bituminous coal or lignite, burn quickly on introduction into the combustor. To avoid a fuel-rich region and the resulting reduced performance, such fuels require more feed points than low-volatile fuels such as bituminous coal or petroleum coke.

Extensive Reading

The Key Factors of Normal Operation of CFB

The key factors of normal operation of CFB are listed below.

(1) High enough circulation rate should be maintained, i. e., the high enough amount of solid particles takes part in the recirculation.

(2) Correct heat release pattern in the dense bed and in the free board, should be kept. In other words, the fractions of heat release and heat absorption in the dense bed and those in the free board should be balanced, thus the temperature of the dense bed and the free board can be controlled at about

850 ℃～900 ℃.

(3) Correct grain size distribution of the coal fed into the bed should be kept. The fraction of grain size lower than 1 mm should be high enough to make the part of the coal entrainted by the flue gas high enough. The fraction of fine grains controls not only the heat release pattern, but also the circulation rate.

(4) The separation efficiency of the separator should be high enough, thus the required circulation rate can be maintained more easily.

The factors mentioned above are inter-related closely. For instance, the fraction of fine particles of the coal fed in is in close relation with the heat release in the dense bed and in the free board above, because if that fraction of fines is higher, more fine coal particles will be entrained by the gas to the free board and burn there, with higher density of carried solid particles, the heat transfer in the free board will be more intensive. At the same time, the heat release rate in the dense bed will become lower.

Furthermore, the efficiency of separation of the separator will influence the circulation rate. If the efficiency is high, the solid particles carried away by the flue gas from the separator will be less. Therefore, the circulation rate can be easily maintained. Or from the other point of view, the fine coal particles will have chance to recycle more times in the recycling track, the combustion of the fine particles will be more complete. Sometimes, excess amount of solid particles in the recycle tract has to be drained to maintain correct rate of recirculation.

It is clear that, the inter relation of these factors is rather complicated. For coal of different characteristics, the fraction of fines should be altered to maintain the correct heat release pattern. For instance, for coal of high volatile content, the volatile matter comes out easily as it is fed into the furnace and is burnt in the free board. With greater fraction of coarse grains can fulfill the requirement of the heat release pattern. On the other hand, for coal with low volatile content, it is important to make the fraction of fine grains higher, so that the heat release in the dense bed will not be too high. The separation efficiency of the separator for very fine particles should be high, thus the other requirements can be easily fulfilled. However, from other point of view, the grain size distribution of the coal fed in is also important to the operation of CFB boiler. If the coal is so prepared, that the most part of the particles are around 1 mm, and the part of very fine particles are low, even if the separation efficiency of the separator is lower for very fine particles, the solid circulation rate can still be maintained.

New Words and Expressions

circulating fluidized bed(CFB)	循环流化床
heat efficiency	热效率
low-grade coal	劣质煤
limestone *n.*	石灰石
desulphuration *n.*	脱硫
air distribution	布风
cyclone *n.*	旋风
separator *n.*	分离器
loop seal	环封
external heat exchanger	外部热交换器
dense region	密相区
dilute region	稀相区
water-cooled	水冷的
primary air	一次风
secondary air	二次风
standpipe	竖管
L-valve	L 形阀
J-valve	J 形阀
return leg	返料腿
mininum voldage	最小空隙度
arching *n.*	架桥作用
air supply system	供气系统
axial-flow type compressor	轴流式压缩机
back-flow	回流
bed expansion	床层膨胀

bed of particles	颗粒床
bed thickness	床层厚度
biological fluidized bed	生物流化床
boiling bed	沸腾床
air bubble	空气泡
recycle system	循环系统
blast *n.*	鼓风
bituminous *a.*	含沥青的
bituminous coal	烟煤（bituminous 含沥青的）
bitumite *n.*	烟煤
cyclone separator	旋风分离器
entrain *v.*	夹带，带走

Part IV

Steam Turbine

● 中文概要
1. 蒸汽式汽轮机的原理、分类和结构组成
2. 汽缸结构
3. 凝汽器的工作原理和结构组成
4. 机组运行特点

4. 1　Introduction

A steam turbine is a device that converts high-pressure steam, produced in a boiler, into mechanical energy that can then be used to produce electricity by forcing blades in a cylinder to rotate and turn a generator shaft. Steam turbine power plants operate on a Rankine cycle.

For a simple steam turbine plant, the first component is the steam boiler which raises steam at the required pressure and temperature for the turbine. The boiler receives feed water at an elevated temperature through various regenerative and heat recuperating apparatuses. In a majority of power plants steam is superheated, in large plants it is reheated once or twice after expanding through some stages. The heat in the furnace is normally provided by burning fossil fuel(e. g. coal, fuel oil, or natural gas). However, the heat can also be provided by biomass, solar energy, or nuclear fuel.

The superheated steam leaving the boiler then enters the steam turbine throttle, part of the heat and pressure energy of steam are changed into mechanical energy by imparting rotary motion to turbine blade wheels. The steam is expanded from a higher to a lower pressure in nozzles or in the blading, and then increases its speed at the expense of its heat and pressure. The speed of the steam is then reduced by doing work on the moving blades and connecting generator to make electricity. After the steam expands through the turbine, it exits the back end of the turbine, where it is cooled and condensed back to water in the surface condenser at a low pressure($0.0035 \sim 0.007$ MPa). This condensate is then returned to the boiler through high-pressure feed pumps for reuse. Heat from the condensing steam is normally rejected from the condenser to a body of water, such as a river or cooling tower.

Modern large steam turbine plants(over 500 MW) have efficiencies approaching $40\% \sim 45\%$. These plants have installed costs between \$ 800/kW and \$ 2,000/kW, depending on environmental permitting requirements.

4. 1. 1   Types of Steam Turbines

Various types of steam turbines can be classified in the following manner.
1. On the basis of flow direction
◆ Axial
◆ Radial
2. On the basis of working principle
◆ Impulse
◆ Reaction
◆ Combined impulse and reaction
3. On the basis of number of stages
◆ Single stage
◆ Multi-stage

4. On the basis of steam entry configuration

◆Full admission

◆Partial admission

5. On the basis of thermodynamic process

◆Condensing turbine

◆Back pressure turbine

◆Extraction turbine

◆Extraction condensing turbine

6. On the basis of rotational speed

◆N=3,000 rpm, f=50 Hz

◆N=3,600 rpm, f=60 Hz

◆N=1,500 rpm

◆Geared units

7. On the basis of applications

◆Electric power generation

◆Industrial

◆Marine

8. On the basis of steam conditions

◆Low-pressure turbines, using steam at pressures of 17. 39 to 28. 98 psi (0. 12 to 0. 2 MPa);

◆Medium-pressure turbines, using steam at pressures up to 28. 98 psi (0. 2 MPa);

◆High-pressure turbine, using steam at pressures of 28. 98 to 2,434. 32 psi(0. 21 to 16. 8 MPa)and higher temperature of 995 ℉(535 ℃)and above;

◆Turbines of supercritical pressures, using steam at pressure of 3,216. 78 psi(22. 2 MPa)and above.

4. 1. 2　Mode of Operation of the Steam Turbine

4. 1. 2. 1　Impulse and Reaction Stage

Stages in which there is no change of static or pressure head of the fluid in the rotor are known as impulse stages. The rotor blades only cause energy transfer without any energy transformation. The energy transformation from pressure or static head to kinetic energy or vice versa takes place only in fixed blades. In contrast, stages in which changes in static or pressure head occur both in the rotor and stator blade passages are known as reaction stages. The rotor experiences both energy transfer and transformation. The degree of reaction of a turbine stage is defined as the ratio of the static or pressure head change occurring in the rotor to the total change across the stage. Therefore reaction turbines are expected to be more efficient on account of the continuously accelerating flow and lower losses.

4.1.2.2 Multi-stage Steam Turbines

It will be seen later that for a given rotor speed only a limited change in the energy level of the fluid can occur in a turbine stage. This holds equally for turbines, compressors, pumps and blowers. Therefore in modern steam turbines not only one impeller is propelled, but several being in a series. Between them idlers are situated, which don't turn. The gas changes its direction passing an idler, in order to perform optimally work again in the next impeller. Turbines with several impellers are called multi-stage. The principle was developed in 1883 by Parsons. As you know, with the cooling gas expands, it is to be paid attention when building steam turbines to a further problem: with the number of passed impellers also the volume increases, which leads to a larger diameter of the impellers. Because of that, multi-level turbines are always conical.

The modern steam turbine is an impulse turbine (no reaction turbine). The advantages, however, to be derived from the use of some multiple impulse elements at the commencement of the turbine are that because there is very little loss in them from leakage, therefore in spite of their low intrinsic efficiency, one or more multiple impulse wheels can in certain cases usefully replace reaction blading.

Generally a multi-stage steam turbine consists of the following essential parts.

(1) A casing usually divided at the horizontal centerline, with the halves bolted together for ease of assembly and disassembly, and containing the stationary blade system.

(2) A rotor with the moving blades on wheels, and with bearing journals on the rotor.

(3) A bearing box in the casing, supporting the shaft.

(4) A governor and valve system for regulating the speed and power of the turbine by controlling the steam flow, and an oil system for lubrication of the bearings and a set of safety devices.

(5) A coupling of some sort to connect with the driven machine.

(6) Pipe connection to a supply of steam at the inlet, and to an exhaust system at the outlet of the casing.

4. 1. 2. 3　Coupling of Several Turbines

In power stations today, different types of turbines are used in a series, e. g. one high-pressure turbines, two medium-pressure turbines and four low-pressure turbines. The typical coupling is shown in Fig. 4-1. This coupling leads to an excellent efficiency(over 40%), which is even better than the efficiency of large diesel engines. This characteristic and the relatively favorable production make the steam turbine competitive in power stations. Coupled with a generator and fired by an atomic reactor, they produce enormously much electric current. The strongest steam turbines achieve today performances of more than 1,000 megawatts.

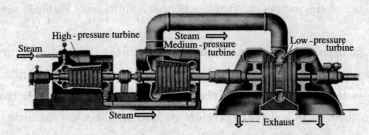

Fig. 4-1　Coupled steam turbine

4. 2　Turbine Construction

4. 2. 1　Casing Construction

A turbine cylinder is essentially a pressure vessel with its weight supported at each end on the horizontal centerline. It is designed to withstand hoop stresses in the transverse plane, and to be very stiff in the longitudinal direction in order to maintain accurate clearances between the stationary and rotating parts of the turbine.

The design is complicated by the need for internal access, all casings being sprit along their horizontal centerline, allowing the rotor to be inserted as a complete assembly. Substantial flanges and bolting are required to withstand the pressure forces at the horizontal joints. The relatively massive flanges respond more slowly to temperature changes than the rest of the casing resulting in different rates of expansion and the setting-up of temperature stresses and distortion, although these are minimized by the application of flange warming steam. Further stress complexities are set up by the gland housing and steam entry and exit passages.

HP and IP casings are of construction and are circular in cross-section to minimize non-membrane stresses. Flanges, bolting, steam penetrations and other features are as far as possible symmetrically arranged to reduce thermal asymmetry and hence distortion. LP casings may be fabricated or a combination of castings and fabrications.

As with all pressure vessels, the integrity of the design is checked after manufacture with a hydraulic pressure test to 150 % of the highest working pressure.

4.2.2　Turbine Rotors

Four different types of rotor construction have been used on large turbine-generator units.

(1) The monobloc or integral rotor, in which the wheels and shaft are formed from a single-piece forging.

(2) The built-up or shrink-on disc rotor, consisting of a forged steel shaft onto which separate forged steel discs are shrunk and keyed.

(3) Drum type rotor manufactured from solid or hollow forgings.

(4) The welded disc rotor. These rotors are not too common in the UK, where they have been applied to LP turbine rotors. Overseas applications have

included HP and IP turbine rotors.

For various reasons, monobloc forgings are preferred but where the size has exceeded the forging capability, the built-up disc construction has been used. The current 660 MW UK designs all have monobloc rotor forgings.

Built-up rotors required very careful attention to shrink fit and location geometries to avoid problems in running and with fatigue cracking. While the discs may have facilitated non-destructive testing(NDT), the NDT capability on monobloc rotors has been developed to meet all the needs. With the monobloc method of construction, the LP rotors are more rigid, resulting in better dynamic behavior. 660 MW plant employs rotors of this construction almost exclusively, and experience has been good.

It was the practice to provide test material from a bore-hole down the forging axis but, as confidence in forging practice and material properties has increased, the central bore has been omitted on some current designs.

Welded rotor construction has the advantage of smaller forging components at the expense of hip integrity welding. The welded design, having been adopted by countries lacking an intrinsic large forging capability, has been successfully applied by them to HP, IP and LP rotors. There are a limited number of welded LP rotors in service in the UK.

High temperature drum-type rotors, manufactured from hollow cylinders bolted to stub shafts, have been prone to differential creep and have been replaced by monobloc drum rotors in current designs. Where constraints on last-stage blading design dictate, double-flow cylinders replace the single-flow design as used in the HP turbine. Double-flow IP and LP turbines are standard for 660 MW designs. With the single-flow HP turbine, the axial thrust has to be balanced to some extent by a "balance piston" to reduce thrust bearing loads; for reaction turbines particularly(with a high pressure drop across the moving blades), the balance piston is of substantial proportions.

In contrast, an HP turbine rotor with impulse blading is characterized by the reduced number of blading stages and larger blading pitch diameter compared with the reaction design. In addition, a very much reduced balance piston is necessary, as the axial thrusts are lower.

4.2.3　Couplings

The need for couplings arises from the limited length of shaft which it is possible to forge in one piece and from the frequent need to use different materials for the various conditions of temperature and stress. The multi-cylinder construction of large turbine-generators necessitates the use of a coupled shaft system.

Couplings are essentially devices for transmitting torque but they may also have to allow relative angular misalignment, transmit axial thrust and ensure axial location or allow relative axial movement. They may be classified as flexible, semiflexible or rigid. On smaller turbine-generators (i. e. up to 120 MW) semiflexible and flexible couplings were commonly used, but for large turbine-generators it is now common practice to use rigid couplings.

4.2.4　Condenser

4.2.4.1　Introduction

The ultimate heat sink for a large thermal power station is the atmosphere. There are various options available, using different processes to achieve the most effective heat sink, and therefore meet the requirements of the condensing plant and cooling water(CW)system.

Typical atmospheric heat dissipation systems:

(1)Process (a) evaporative cooling, associated with closed systems(cooling towers)for heat dissipation.

(2)Process (b) heated water discharges, associated with direct cooled systems (river or seawater)for heat dissipation.

When considering a new site for a power station, it is important at the planning stages to ensure that it has adequate cooling water facilities. With increasingly high station output and unit rating, the choice of location is narrowed by the necessity to match available water resources. This along with equally important factors, such as type of fuel and selection of steam conditions, are the major features considered when assessing the suitability of any site.

In order for a steam power station to operate an efficient close cycle, the condensing plant, CW system, and associated pumps must extract the maximum quantity of heat from the exhaust steam of the LP turbines.

The primary functions of the condensing plant:

(1) To provide the lowest economic heat rejection temperature for the steam cycle.

(2) To convert the exhaust steam to water for reuse in the feed cycle.

(3) To collect the useful residual heat from the drains of the turbine feed-heating plant, and other auxiliaries.

The aim of the CW system is to maintain a supply of cooling medium to extract the necessary heat, in order that the condensing plant can meet its objectives. It achieves this by the use of effective screening equipment, circulating water pumps, valves, and(where necessary) cooling towers.

The screening plant must remove any debris from the cooling water which is large enough to block the condenser or auxiliary cooler tubes. It must be easy to keep clean, even during periods of excessive debris.

The cooling water(CW)pumps must circulate the water against system resistance, or pumping head, all conditions encountered at a particular site. To ensure efficient and flexible CW pump operation, valves are usually provided to allow any combination of pumps, condensers and cooling towers to operate together.

In the heated water discharge direct-cooled system, the cooling water(river or seawater) is used once and then discharged. In the evaporative-cooled closed cooling tower and mixed cooling systems, the cooling towers transfer heat from the plant to the atmosphere and the cooled water is re-circulated. In this case the water requirements are for make-up and purge purposes only.

In addition to the condenser satisfying the primary functions, its design must also be capable of meeting the following objectives:

(1) To provide the turbine with the most economic back pressure consistent with the seasonal variations in CW temperature or the heat sink temperature of the CW system.

(2) To effectively prevent chemical contamination of the condensate either from CW leakage or from inadequate steam space gas removal and condensate de-aeration.

54

4.2.4.2　Surface Condenser

The condenser is of the high efficiency surface type. A condenser is composed of casings, tube plates, cooling tubes, etc(Fig. 4-2). For a typical condenser, adequate space is provided between the shell and tube nest to allow free access of the steam to the whole periphery of the nest.

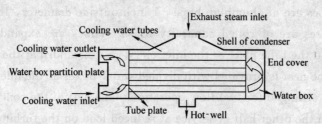

Fig. 4-2　Internal structure of a condenser

The steam entering the tube nest over the whole periphery reduces the velocity to a minimum and this, together with the central air removal which provides the shortest path, reduces the pressure drop to a minimum and so ensures a high average rate of heat transmission. Air is withdrawn from the coldest region of the tube nest, achieving maximum cooling of air and vapor.

A feature of this type of air withdrawal is that maximum condensation takes place where the air concentration is least, resulting in minimum absorption of air by the condensate, the oxygen content being reduced to a negligible value.

Briefly summarized, the main advantages of the design of condenser are as follows:

1. Improved rate of heat transmission

The more effective use of the cooling surface enables a given performance to be attained with a smaller tube area, or a better performance with a given area of cooling surface.

2. High condensate temperature

By surrounding the whole of the tube nest, the steam comes into intimate contact with the falling condensate and, as a result, no under-cooling of the condensate takes place. The condensate leaves the condenser at a temperature slightly above that of the exhaust steam thus reducing the expenditure of heat to be provided by the boiler.

3. Improved ejector performance

The condenser design imposes a fighter duty on the ejectors and enables the size of these to be reduced, with a decrease in the steam or power required for operation.

For construction in a typical condenser, some of the features are as follows: tubes are of aluminum brass, 1 inch outside diameter, 18 s. w. g. and the tube-plates are of rolled admiralty brass. Tubes are expanded and bell-mouthed into the tube-plate at the inlet ends, and expanded at the outlet ends.

The tube nest is provided with divided water boxes at the inlet and the reverse end is arranged for two flow operation. One half of the condenser can be cleaned with the other half in service at reduced load on the turbine. The usual fittings are provided.

4.2.4.3 Air Extraction Equipment

The objectives of the air extraction plant.

(1) To remove air which has leaked into the condenser via flanges and glands effectively.

(2) To remove other incondensable gases that are present in the steam exhausting from the LP turbines.

It is important that both are removed from the condenser, as their presence in any quantity impairs the heat transfer performance of the condenser. Conversely, excessive air extraction capacity should be avoided.

The air extraction plant must be capable of functioning under two regimes: one when normal operation, the other when raising vacuum on the turbine-generator unit.

When raising vacuum, the air extraction equipment is faced with a large quantity of air which must be removed, and must therefore have the capacity for reducing the pressure in the condenser quickly to a level which allows the turbine to be started.

The main development of air extraction equipment for large condensers has evolved through the use of air extraction pumps. Steam-jet air ejectors were in common use, however, for the higher pressure and temperature cycles adopted today, these have proved to be less economic than air pumps, both in capital and running costs.

The liquid-ring type air pump is commonly adopted. This is essentially a centrifugal displacement pump. A multi-blade impeller revolves within an offset casing which is partially full of water. The rotating impeller throws the liquid outwards, resulting in a solid ring of liquid revolving in the casing at the same speed as the rotor, but following the shape of the casing. This alternately causes the liquid to enter and recede from the inter-blade spaces on the impeller. The provision of inlet and outlet ports enables the pump action to be used for evacuation of air from the condenser. The advantages of this type of pump are that it is simple and reliable, with large clearances on rotating parts, and no valves or pistons.

4.3   Operating Characteristics

Steam turbines, especially smaller units, leak steam around blade rows and out the end seals. When end is at a low pressure, air can also leak into the system. The leakages cause less power to be produced than expected, and the water has to be treated to avoid boiler and turbine material problems. Air that has leaked in needs to be removed, which is usually done by a compressor removing non-condensable gases from the condenser. Because of the high pressures used in steam turbines, the casing is quite thick, and consequently steam turbines exhibit large thermal inertia. Steam turbines must be warmed up and cooled down slowly to minimize the differential expansion between the rotating blades and the stationary parts. Large steam turbines can take over ten hours to warm up. While smaller units have more rapid startup times, steam turbines differ appreciably from reciprocating engines, which start up rapidly, and from gas turbines, which can start up in a moderate amount of time and load follow with reasonable rapidity. Steam turbine applications usually operate continuously for extended periods, although the steam fed to the unit and the power delivered may vary (slowly) during such periods of continuous operation.

Extensive Reading

Types of Steam Turbines

Steam turbines differ from reciprocating engines and gas turbines in that the fuel is burned in a piece of equipment, the boiler, which is separate from the power generation equipment, the steam turbogenerator. As mentioned previously, this separation of functions enables steam turbines to operate with an enormous variety of fuels.

For size up to (approximately) 40 MW, horizontal industrial boilers are built. This enables rail, car, ship, with considerable cost savings and improved quality as the cost and quality of factory labor is usually both lower in cost and greater in quality than field labor. Large shop assembled boilers are typically capable of firing only gas or distillate oil, as there is inadequate residence time for complete combustion of most solid and residual fuels in such designs. Large field-erected industrial boilers firing solid and residual fuels bear a resemblance to utility boilers except for the actual solid fuel injection. Large boilers usually burn pulverized coal, however intermediate and small boilers burning coal or solid fuel employ various types of solids feeders.

Types of Steam Turbines

The primary type of turbine used for central power generation is the condensing turbine. These power-only utility turbines exhaust directly to condensers that maintain vacuum conditions at the discharge of the turbine. An array of tubes, cooled by river, lake, or cooling tower water, condenses the steam into (liquid) water. The cooling water condenses the steam turbine exhaust steam in the condenser creating the condenser vacuum. As a small amount of air leaks into the system when it is below atmospheric pressure, a relatively small compressor removes non-condensable gases from the condenser. Non-condensable gases include both air and a small amount of the corrosion byproduct of the water-iron reaction, hydrogen.

The condensing turbine processes result in maximum power and electrical generation efficiency from the steam supply and boiler fuel. The power output of condensing turbines is sensitive to ambient conditions.

CHP applications use two types of steam turbines, non-condensing and extraction.

Non-Condensing (Back-pressure) Turbine

Fig. 4-3 shows the non-condensing turbine (also referred to as a back-pressure turbine) exhausts its entire flow of steam to the industrial process or facility steam mains at conditions close to the process heat requirements.

Usually, the steam sent into the mains is not much above saturation temperature. The term "back-pressure" refers to turbines that exhaust steam at atmospheric pressures and above. The specific CHP application establishes the discharge pressure. 50, 150, and 250 psi are the most typical pressure levels for steam distribution systems. District heating systems most often use the lower pressures, and industrial processes use the higher pressures. Industrial processes often include further expansion for mechanical drives, using small steam turbines for driving heavy equipment that runs continuously for long periods. Power generation capability reduces significantly when steam is used at appreciable pressure rather than being expanded to vacuum in a condenser. Discharging steam into a steam distribution system at 150 psi can sacrifice slightly more than half the power that could be generated when the inlet steam conditions are 750 psi and 800 °F, typical of small steam turbine systems.

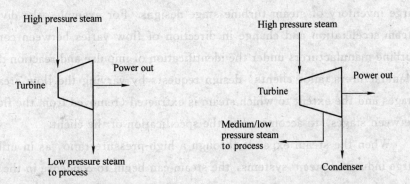

Fig. 4-3   Non-Condensing steam turbine   Fig. 4-4   Extraction steam turbine

Extraction Turbine

The extraction turbine has opening(s) in its casing for extraction of a portion of the steam at some intermediate pressure before condensing the remaining steam. Fig. 4-4 illustrates the extracted steam may be used for process purposes in a CHP facility or for feedwater heating as is the case in most utility power plants.

The steam extraction pressure may or may not be automatically regulated. Regulated extraction permits more steam to flow through the turbine to generate additional electricity during periods of low thermal demand by the CHP system. In utility type steam turbines, there may be several extraction points, each at a different pressure corresponding to a different temperature. The facility's specific needs for steam and power over time determine the extent to which steam in an extraction turbine is extracted for use in the process.

In large, often complex, industrial plants, additional steam may be admitted (flows into the casing and increases the flow in the steam path) to the steam turbine. Often this happens when using multiple boilers at different pressure, because of their historical existence. These steam turbines are referred to as admission turbines. At steam extraction and admission locations, there are usually steam flow control valves that add to the steam and control system cost.

Numerous mechanical design features increase efficiency, provide for operation over a range of conditions, simplify manufacture and repair, and achieve other practical purposes. The long history of steam turbine has resulted in a large inventory of steam turbine stage designs. For example, the division of steam acceleration and change in direction of flow varies between competing turbine manufacturers under the identification of impulse and reaction designs. Manufacturers tailor clients' design requests by varying the flow area in the stages and the extent to which steam is extracted (removed from the flow path between stages) to accommodate the specification of the client.

When the steam expands through a high-pressure ratio, as in utility and large industrial steam systems, the steam can begin to condense in the turbine when the temperature of the steam drops below the saturation temperature at that pressure. If water drops form in the turbine, blade erosion occurs from the drops impact on the blades. At this point in the expansion the steam is sometimes returned to the boiler and reheated to high temperature and then returned to the turbine for further (safe) expansion. In a few large, high pressure, utility steam systems install double reheat systems.

With these choices the designers of the steam supply system and the steam turbine have the challenge of creating a system design which delivers the (seasonally varying) power and steam which presents the most favorable business opportunity to the plant owners.

Between the power (only) output of a condensing steam turbine and the power and steam combination of a back-pressure steam turbine essentially any ratio of power to heat output can be supplied. Back-pressure steam turbines can be obtained with a variety of back pressures, further increasing the variability of the power-to-heat ratio.

Design Characteristics

Custom design: Steam turbines are designed to match CHP design pressure and temperature requirements and to maximize electric efficiency while providing the desired thermal output.

Thermal output: Steam turbines are capable of operating over a broad range of steam pressures. Utility steam turbines operate with inlet steam pressures up to 3,500 psig and exhaust vacuum conditions as low as one inch of Hg (absolute). Steam turbines are custom designed to deliver the thermal requirements of the CHP applications through use of back-pressure or extraction steam at appropriate pressures and temperatures.

Fuel flexibility: Steam turbines offer a wide range of fuel flexibility using a variety of fuel sources in the associated boiler or other heat source, including coal, oil, natural gas, wood and waste products.

Reliability and life: Steam turbine life is extremely long. When properly operated and maintained (including proper control of boiler water chemistry), steam turbines are extremely reliable, only requiring overhauls every several years. They require controlled thermal transients to minimize different expansion of the parts as the massive casing slowly heats up.

Size range: Steam turbines are available in size from under 100 kW to over 250

MW. In the multi-megawatt size range, industrial and utility steam turbine designations merge, with the same turbine (high-pressure section) able to serve both industrial and small utility applications.

Emissions: Emissions are dependent upon the fuel used by the boiler or other steam source, boiler furnace combustion section design and operation, and built-in and add-on boiler exhaust cleanup systems.

New Words and Expressions

steam turbine	汽轮机
high-pressure(HP) cylinder	高压汽缸
condensing steam turbine	凝汽式汽轮机
tube plate	管板
intermediate-pressure(IP) cylinder	中压汽缸
hot-well	热水井
low-pressure(LP) cylinder	低压汽缸
turbine rotor	汽轮机转子
steam seal gland/steam sealing	汽封
blade/bucket n.	叶片
nozzle n.	喷嘴
condenser n.	冷凝器
shaft n.	轴
condenser throat	冷凝器喉部
condensate pump	凝结水泵
low-pressure feed-water heater	低压给水加热器
deaerator n.	除氧器
high-pressure feed-water heater	高压给水加热器
feed-water pump	给水泵
deaerated water tank	除氧水箱
drain pump	疏水泵
drain flash tank	疏水扩容器
baffle plate	挡板
vaccum pump	真空泵

industrial water pump/service water pump	工业水泵
main steam system	主蒸汽系统
reheat steam syetem	再热蒸汽系统
steam extraction system	抽汽系统
main steam piping	主蒸汽管道
vaccum system	真空系统
condensate system	凝结水系统
feed-water system	给水系统
circulating water system	循环水系统
steam extraction pipe	抽汽管道
steam header	供汽联箱
circulating water piping	循环水管道
cooling water piping	冷却水管道
feed-water piping	给水管道
recirculating water piping	再循环水管道
drain valve	疏水阀
rotating speed/revolution speed	转速
thermal efficiency/heat efficiency	热效率
temperature difference	温差
opening n.	开启
closing n.	关闭
cold reheated steam pressure	再热蒸汽冷段压力
hot reheated steam pressure	再热蒸汽热段压力
starting up	启动
shutting down	停止
hot reheated steam temperature	再热蒸汽热段温度
cold reheated steam temperature	再热蒸汽冷段温度
cleaning n.	清洗
inspection/examination n.	检查
routine inspection	巡检
low-pressure cylinder exhaust steam flow	低压缸排汽流量
flange heating	法兰加热
bolt heating	螺栓加热

normal condition	正常状态
operation n.	操作
disassembly n.	解体
assembly n.	组装
maintenance n.	检修
crack n.	裂纹
wall thickness	壁厚
alignment n.	找中心
flow n.	流量
tube bundle	管束
steam extraction capacity	抽汽量

Part V

Thermal Power Plant

● **中文概要**

1. 热电厂设备组成及工作流程
2. 给水流程图
3. 热电厂给水加热、除氧、回热等系统
4. 热力参数

5.1 The Modern Steam Power Plant

5.1.1 Introduction

A power plant, of whatever variety, consists of three essential elements: the heat source, the heat utilizer, and the waste heat reservoir or refrigerator. To generate power or produce useful work, it is required that heat be supplied to a working fluid, from the heat source. The utilizer is required to convert a portion of the heat supplied to the working fluid into useful power. Since, by the second law of thermodynamics, not all the heat can be converted to useful power, a refrigerator is required to dispose of the remainder of the heat.

Fig. 5-1 is a diagram of a modem steam plant, showing most of the essential elements. It may be divided into two main halves. One half consists of the boiler or heat source and its auxiliaries; the other, the turbine cycle, consists of turbine, generator, condenser, pumps and feed-water heaters. the turbine cycle, which includes not only the heat utilizer but also the refrigerator, will occupy the major part of our attention in this text.

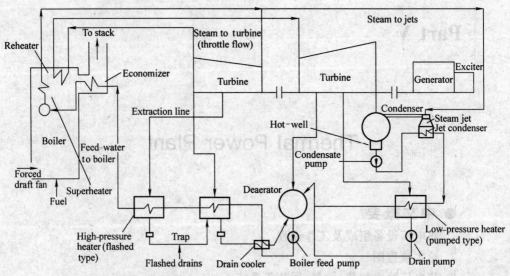

Fig. 5-1 Flow diagram of a typical steam power plant

At first considering the boiler plant involved in the cycle, feed-water is supplied to the boiler drum, where water is boiled and converted into dry saturated steam. This dry steam is further superheated and then fed to the HP cylinder of the turbine. The steam expands in the turbine giving up heat energy, a high proportion of which is transferred into work energy on the turbine shaft. The shaft turns an electrical generator which produces electric power. Steam leaving the HP cylinder returns to the boiler, where it is reheated. The reheated steam is further expanded in the IP and LP cylinders, before passing into the condenser. In the condenser, which is a large surface-type heat exchanger, the steam is condensed by transferring its latent heat of vaporization to the cooling water (CW). The main steam, having been condensed in the condenser, is now in a liquid state at a very low pressure and approximately saturation temperature. This water drains from the condenser, where it enters the hot-well. The water in the hot-well is pumped by the condensate extraction pump through the low pressure feed-heating system to another pump, the boiler feed pump.

In a modern regenerative cycle, some of the steam passing through the turbine cylinders is bled from a series of extraction belts located after selected moving blade stages and fed to the condenser and feed-water heaters. This steam is used to heat the condensate in the LP heaters and the feed-water in the HP heaters, which are of a surface type.

The boiler feed pump increases the water pressure to a level in excess of the drum pressure, to provide for the pressure loss in the boiler circuit and HP feed-heating train. The cycle is now complete.

5.1.2 Boiler and Main Steam System

Boiler and main steam system in Fig. 5-2. Considering first the boiler half of the cycle, feed-water is supplied through an economizer to the boiler drum. The economizer reclaims part of the heat in the stack gases and transfers it to the feed-water, thus decreasing the heat to be supplied in the boiler while reducing the temperature of the stack gases. In the boiler drum, the water is boiled and converted to dry and saturated steam, which enters the superheater where the heat of superheat is added. The major part of the steam leaving the superheater is taken to the steam turbine. In many plants some of the steam is bled off for using in a steam-jet air ejector. Steam passing through the steam turbine produces mechanical power on the turbine shaft, which drives the alternator where electrical energy is generated for distribution. On passing through the turbine in the modern regenerative cycle, some of the steam is bled from the turbine at a series of seven or eight openings(more or less), for using in feed-water heaters. Approximately 70% to 75% of the steam supplied to the turbine at the throttle continues all the way through the turbine to the exhaust hood, where it passes to the condenser.

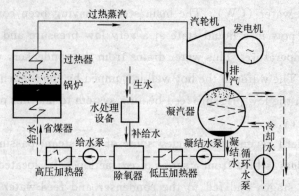

Fig. 5-2　火力发电厂的汽水系统流程图(此图便于中英文对照)

5.1.3　Condensate System

In the condenser which is a large surface-type heat exchanger, the steam is condensed by transferring its latent heat to circulating water taken from a nearby river or lake. The circulating water is supplied to the condenser by circulating water pumps, either motor or steam turbine driven. Since tremendous quantities of steam pass into the condenser, it is unavoidable that a certain proportion of non-condensable gases accompanies it. In order that a very low pressure, approximating a perfect vacuum, may be maintained in the condenser, these "non-condensable" must be removed from the shell of the condenser. Usually they are removed by means of a steam-jet air ejector, consisting principally of a nozzle through which steam passes at high velocity and in which the non-condensable vapors are entrained. The steam passing through the nozzle (motive steam) and the non-condensable gases mechanically entrained in it are then taken to a heat-transfer device known as an after-condenser, where the steam is condensed at atmospheric pressure and the non-condensable vapors are vented to atmosphere. The steam-jet air ejector, built in either one or two stages, is essentially a compressor for raising the pressure of the non-condensable vapors from an almost perfect vacuum to atmospheric pressure, to dispose of them.

The main steam, having been condensed in the condenser, is now in the form of liquid water at a very low pressure and approximately saturation temperature. This water drains by gravity to the bottom of the condenser, where it enters a hot-well. Usually the level of the water in the hot-well is maintained by a control applied to the hot-well pump. The hot-well pump removes the water from the hot-well and pumps it through the lower part of the feedwater heating system to another pump, the boiler feed pump. The water discharged from the hot-well pump is taken first to a low-pressure heater in which heat is supplied by the lowest pressure extraction. The low-pressure heater is equipped with a drain pump, the duty of which is to remove the drains(formed by the condensing steam)from the heater and to pump them into the main condensate line, beyond the heater. This type of heater is known as a pumped heater.

5. 1. 4　Deaerator and Feed System

From the low-pressure heater the condensate passes to a deaerating heater. The deaerating heater, a direct contact type, serves as a means of boiling the condensate to eliminate any entrained oxygen. Removal of oxygen in the deaerating heater is based on the principle that solubility of non-condensable gases in water is greatly reduced as the temperature of the water approaches the boiling point. Steam extracted from the turbine supplies the heat required to raise to the boiling point, the temperature of the condensate entering the deaerator. The non-condensable gases discharged from the surface of the water must be removed. Normally the deaerator is operated at a pressure higher than atmospheric, so that these gases may be vented through a vent condenser. Usual practice is to cool the vent condenser with incoming condensate, to cool the non-condensable gases, and simultaneously to condense the steam, some of which unavoidably escapes from the deaerator with the gases. By proper design of the vent condenser, the steam may be condensed and permitted to drain back into the deaerator, while the non-condensable gases are vented to atmosphere through an orifice.

Occasionally in the original design it may be planned that the deaerator operate at pressures below atmospheric. Even when the full load design pressure is considerably higher than atmospheric,it is found that at the lighter loads the pressure becomes sub-atmospheric. It is then essential that the non-condensables continue to be removed from the deaerator, and a steam-jet ejector is necessary for accomplishing this result. The expense and complication in operation occasioned by Such an installation make it undesirable. For this reason it is common practice to provide for the shifting of extraction stages at light loads so that the deaerator steam supply is furnished by the next-hight loads and the next-higher extraction point. A simple arrangement is to install a crossover pipe containing a controlling valve, with a check valve in the lower-pressure extraction line before its junction with this crossover pipe. Such an installation opening of the valve in the crossover line automatically supplies higher-pressure steam to the deaerator, and the check valve closes, preventing backflow to the lower extraction stage.

In many power plants a surge tank containing reserve stored water is connected in parallel with the deaerator. The function of the surge tank is to serve as an emergency supply of distilled water in the event of failure of other sources, or as a reservoir for excess water during load changes, etc. Normally the storage capacity of the deaerator is sufficient to operate the power plant for several minutes, but most designers consider it wise to augment this storage capacity with a large surge tank.

In the majority of large power plants the boiler-feed pump is connected to the discharge of the deaerator. Since the water in the deaerator is at its boiling point, it is essential that the boiler-feed pump is located a considerable distance (usually 20 ft. (6m.) or more) below the deaerator, to avoid flashing of the water in the boiler-feed pump suction. Water leaving the deaerator goes to the boiler-feed pump suction and is pumped into the next higher heater. In Fig. 5-1 this heater is shown as a drain cooler heater, that is, a heater the drains from which pass through a heat exchange(drain cooler), giving up heat to the incoming condensate. After leaving this heater, the condensate goes to the top or high-pressure heater, in which the condensate is heated to the final feedwater temperature. In Fig. 5-1 the top heater is shown as a flashed heater, so called because its drains are permitted to pass through a controlling orifice or trap to the next-lower heater where part of the saturated water flashes into steam. This arrangement eliminates the use of drain pumps and drain coolers, but it causes a considerable thermodynamic loss. The final feedwater temperature leaving the top heater is in the order of 148.9 ℃ ~ 232.2 ℃ in large modem power plants, and occasionally higher.

Illustrated in Fig. 5-1 are examples of the four types of heater, namely the flashed heater, the drain-cooler heater, the deaerating or contact heater, and the pumped heater.

5.1.4 Reheat Cycle

The desire for further increases in cycle conditions and consequent increases in cycle efficiency, which led to the addition of steam reheat during turbine expansion.

In the reheat cycle, steam at a given initial temperature is partially expanded through the turbine doing some work, and then is fed back to the boiler, where it is reheated to original temperature. The heated steam is then fed through the remainder of the turbine before being condensed.

The reheat cycle incorporates an improvement in thermal efficiency over the superheat cycle.

The reheat cycle benefits from reduced wetness in the turbine exhaust, but presents an increased capital outlay in terms of reheater pipework to, from and within the boiler. The turbine is usually split into HP and LP cylinders to avoid the high thermal gradients which would be introduced between stages of reheat on a singlecylinder machine.

5.1.5 Regenerative Feedheating

To complete the cycle development of the steam cycle, the inclusion of regenerative feedheating must be discussed. Physically, a proportion of the steam is bled from various points on the turbine, which is then condensed to heat feed-water on its return to the boiler. The improvement in thermal efficiency for a simple Rankine cycle is by virtue of the bled-steam releasing all of its heat to the feed-water, and little or none to the condenser. There will be a small loss of work available from the bled-steam not expanding in the turbine, however, this loss is out-weighted by the gain in cycle efficiency.

The greater the number of feed-heaters installed, the greater the improvement in thermal efficiency. However, the incremental gain for each additional feed-heater reduces as the number of heaters increases.

5.2　Performance Characteristics of CHP

5.2.1　Electrical Efficiency

The electrical generating efficiency of standard steam turbine power plants varies from a high of 37% HHV (measured on a higher heating value basis) for large, electric utility plants designed for the highest practical annual capacity factor, to under 10% HHV for small, simple plants which make electricity as a by-product of delivering steam to processes or district heating systems. Steam turbine thermodynamic efficiency (isentropic efficiency) refers to the ratio of power actually generated from the turbine to what would be generated by a perfect turbine with no internal losses using steam at the same inlet conditions and discharging to the same downstream pressure (actual enthalpy drop divided by the isentropic enthalpy drop). Turbine thermodynamic efficiency is not to be confused with electrical generating efficiency, which is the ratio of net power generated to total fuel input to the cycle. Steam turbine thermodynamic efficiency measures, how efficiently the turbine extracts power from the steam itself.

Multistage (moderate to high-pressure ratio) steam turbines have thermodynamic efficiencies that vary from 65% for small (under 1,000 kW) units to over 90% for large industrial and utility sized units. Small, single stage steam turbines can have efficiencies as low as 50%. When a steam turbine exhausts to a CHP (combined heat and power) application, the turbine efficiency is not as critical as in a power only condensing mode. The majority of the energy not extracted by the steam turbine satisfies the thermal load. (Power only applications waste the exhaust turbine steam energy in condensers.)

Table 5-1 summarizes performance characteristics for typical boiler or steam CHP systems in the 500 kW to 15 MW size range.

5.2.2　CHP System Efficiency

Steam turbine CHP systems generally have low power to heat ratios, typically in the 0.05 to 0.2 range. This is because electricity is a byproduct of heat generation, with the system optimized for steam production. Hence, while electrical efficiency of steam turbine CHP system may seem low, because the primary objective is to produce large amounts of steam. The effective electrical efficiency of steam turbine systems, however, is generally high, because almost all the energy difference between the high-pressure boiler output and the lower-pressure turbine output is converted to electricity. This means that total CHP system efficiencies are generally high and approach the boiler efficiency level. Steam boiler efficiencies range from $70\% \sim 85\%$ HHV depending on boiler type and age, fuel, duty cycle, application, and steam conditions.

Table 5-1 Boiler/Steam Turbine CHP System Cost and Performance Characteristics

Cost & Performance Characteristics	System 1	Syestem 2	System 3
Steam turbine parameters			
Nominal electricity capacity (kW)	500	3,000	15,000
Turbine type	Back pressure	Back pressure	Back pressure
Equipment cost ($/kW)	540	225	205
Total installed cost ($/kW)	918	385	349
Turbine isentropic efficiency (%)	50	70	80
Generator/gearbox efficiency (%)	94	94	97
Steam flow (lbs/hr)	21,500	126,000	450,000
Inlet pressure (psig)	500	600	700
Inlet temperature (°F)	550	575	650
Outlet pressure (psig)	50	150	150
Outlet temperature (°F)	298	366	366
CHP system parameters			
Cost & Performance Characteristics	System 1	Syestem 2	System 3
Boiler efficiency (%), HHV	80	80	80
CHP electric efficiency (%), HHV	6.4	6.9	9.3
Fuel input (MMBtu/hr)	26.7	147.4	549.0
Steam to process (MMBtu/hr)	19.6	107.0	386.6
Steam to process (kW)	5,740	31,352	113,291

Total CHP efficiency (%), HHV	79.6	79.5	79.7
Power/heat ratio	0.09	0.10	0.13
Net heat rate (Btu/kWh)	4,515	4,568	4,388
Effective electrical efficiency (%), HHV	75.6	75.1	77.8

5.2.3 Performance and Efficiency Enhancements

In industrial steam turbine systems, business conditions determine the requirements and relative values of electric power and steam. Plant system engineers then decide the extent of efficiency enhancing options to incorporate in terms of their incremental effects on performance and plant cost, and select appropriate steam turbine inlet and exhaust conditions. Often the steam turbine is going into a system that already exists and is being modified, so that a number of steam system design parameters are already determined by previous decisions, which exist as system hardware characteristics.

As the stack temperature of the boiler exhaust combustion products still contain some heat, trade-off occur regarding the extent of investment in heat reclamation equipment for the sake of efficiency improvement. Often the stack exhaust temperature is set at a level where further heat recovery would results in condensation of corrosive chemical species in the stack, with consequential deleterious effects on stack life and safety.

Extensive Reading

Classification of Heaters

The heat balance of modem steam plants is not well standardized with respecting to the arrangement of heaters used. In broad classification, all heaters are classed as either surface or contact type. In the surface type, so called because of its use of indirect heating surface, the condensate flows through the tubes and extraction steam enters the shell side of the heater. Either finned tubes or plain tubes are used, although the plain are by far the common. In the surface type heater the heating surface must be arranged to permit free thermal expansion of the tube bundle when heated by extraction steam. Expansion may be taken care of either by the floating-head type of construction or by use of bent hairpin-type tubes. It is customary for the surface type heater to be used in the higher pressure portions of the feed-water heating cycle, because at this end of the cycle condensate is under full boiler pressure or higher and is more easily contained within tubes than within the shell of a contact-type heater.

The contact-type heater is most frequently used as a deaerator. It consists of a large steel shell, having considerable condensate-storage capacity, in which both steam and condensate are completely intermingled. The condensate is supplied to the contact-type heater through a vent condenser and is permitted to pass to the bottom of heater by spilling over a series of trays. The passage of steam through the sheet of condensate running over the sides of the trays assures complete intermixing of steam and water, and heating of condensate to the saturation temperature corresponding to the pressure in the heater. It is well known that, when water is raised to its boiling point, the solubility of any permanent gases contained within the water is greatly decreased, causing these gases to leave the water. The deaerator in a power plant cycle has a double function: it heats the water through an appreciable temperature rise, 60°F or 70 °F(15. 6 or 21. 1 ℃), and at the same time it causes the water to reach its saturation temperature. This liberates the non-condensable gases from the condensate. These non-condensable gases then pass through the vent condenser, where water vapor is condensed and the gases are discharged to atmosphere.

Occasionally contact-type heaters are used in the low-pressure section of a feed-water heating system, but they are the exceptions rather than the roles. At least one large turbine installation, however, uses contact heaters for all extractions. The desirability (from a purely thermal standpoint) of such an arrangement is unquestioned, but its thermodynamic gain must be balanced against the necessity for a separate pump at each contact heater. (The fact that each pump must be able to handle full condensate flow of the power plant represents a maintenance expense and reliability hazard.)

New Words and Expressions

abnormal operating conditions	异常运行情况
alternator *n.*	交流发电机
AC auxiliary oil pump	交流辅助油泵
back-up	备品,辅助的
advanced gas-cooled reactor(AGR)	改进气冷反应堆
baffle *n.*	挡板,反射板
bearing *n.*	轴承(座),支承(座,架)
bled-steam	抽汽
boiler feed-water pump	锅炉给水泵
chamber *n.*	燃烧室,小室,箱,容器
check valve *n.*	逆止阀,单向阀
chest *n.*	箱,柜,室
circulating water	循环水
condensate extraction pump	凝结水泵
contact-type heater	混合式加热器
controlling valve	控制阀,调节阀
cooling water(CW)	冷却水
crossover *n.*	跨越,交叉,交叠管路
cycle efficiency	循环效率
cylinder *n.*	圆筒,圆柱体,汽缸
desuperheater *n.*	减温器,过热蒸汽冷却器
disc *n.*	圆盘,片,轮盘,叶轮
drain *n.*	排水管,排水,疏水
drain cooler heater	疏水冷却器
drain pump	疏水泵
duty *n.*	功率,负荷,工作状态
economizer *n.*	省煤器
ejector *n.*	喷射器,抽汽器
enthalpy *n.*	焓
exhaust conditions	排汽参数

76

extraction point	抽汽点
extraction steam	抽汽
feed pump	给水泵
ferritic *a.*	铁素体的,铁酸盐的
finned *a.*	有加强筋的,有散热片的
fire-resistant fluid(FRF)	抗燃油
flashed heater	疏水逐级自流加热器
flashing	瞬间汽化,闪蒸
floating-head	(换热器的)浮头,浮动盖
full load	满负荷
generator *n.*	发电机,传感器
gland *n.*	密封装置,汽封装置
heater *n.*	加热器
hot start	热启动
hydraulic *a.*	水力的,水压的,水力学的
initial temperature	初温
labyrinth *n.*	迷宫式轴封
load *n.*	负荷,载荷,负载
lubricating oil	润滑油
main steam	主汽
mechanical power	机械功
orifice *n.*	孔,口,节流孔,孔板
output *n.*	输出量,功率,容量
perfect vacuum	最佳真空
pipework *n.*	管路
pitch *n.*	节距,螺距,坡度,斜度
pitch diameter	平均直径,节圆直径
power station	电厂
pump *n.*	泵,抽水机
pumped heater	带疏水泵的加热器
regenerative cycle	回热循环
reliability *n.*	可靠性,安全性
run-up	加速

sealing *n.*	密封,封闭,焊封
shaft *n.*	轴,竖井,烟囱,炉身
shutdown	关闭,断开,停工
stack *n.*	烟囱,(高炉)炉身
stack gases	(烟囱中的)烟气
steam jet/ai ejector	射汽抽汽器
stop valves	断流阀,截止阀
suction *n.*	吸力,吸管,吸口
supercritical plant	超临界机组
surface-type heater	表面式加热器
tank *n.*	槽,箱,柜,罐,池
thermal efficiency	热效率
thermal fatigue	热疲劳
throttle *n.*	节流阀
trap *n.*	汽水分离器
tray *n.*	盘,浅盘,底盘
turbine-generator unit	汽轮发电机组
turning gear	盘车
ultra-supercritical	超超临界
vacuum *n.*	真空,真空装置
a.	真空的
vent *n.*	口,孔,通道,通风口

Part Ⅵ

Instrumentation and Control
in Thermal Power Station

● 中文概要
1. 热工过程自动控制理论
2. 自动控制仪表和参数
3. 锅炉汽包水位控制
4. 主蒸汽压力控制

6.1　Introduction

Instrumentation and Control(I&C) is an integral part of a coal-fired power station. A modern, advanced I&C system plays a major role in the profitable operation of a plant by achieving maximum availability, reliability, flexibility, maintainability and efficiency. These systems can also assist in maintaining emissions compliance. The I&C chain begins with sensors that detect meas-

79

ured values. Controllers receive these values, upon which a control strategy is activated. The response, where and when required, moves in final actuating control elements to modify the affect process. This loop repeats over and over during plant operation through a complex and multi-level communications schemes.

"Smart" field devices, including sensors and actuators, continue to be developed in order to simplify and improve the control process. The two main control platforms that are used in coal-fired power stations are the distributed control system (DCS) and the programmable logic control (PLC). Personal computer (PC) based hardware and software have only recently been introduced in power plant control. With the fast development, increasing power and reduced cost of personal computers, PC-based control is expected to become a further platform for future development and growth. Today new coal-fired power plants are, in general, built with modern, advanced DCS/PLC and a large number of existing coal-fired power stations have been retrofitted with advanced digital systems in many countries, throughout the world.

6. 2　Application of Automatic Control in Thermal Power Station

Today, a power plant control system is most often an integrated package with demand requirements applied simultaneously to the boiler, turbine and major auxiliary equipment. This minimizes the number of complex interactions between subsystems.

Various types of boiler control systems for fossil fuel boilers include:
◆ Boiler instrumentation
◆ Combustion(fuel and air)control
◆ Steam temperature control for superheater and reheater outlet
◆ Drum level and feedwater control
◆ Burner sequence control and management systems
◆ Bypass and start up
◆ Systems to integrate all of the above with the turbine and electric generator control
◆ Data processing, event recording, trend recording and display

♦ Performance calculation and analysis

♦ Alarm annunciation system

♦ Management information system

♦ Unit trip system

6. 2. 1　Feed-water Control

Drum water level is one of the most important measurements for safe and reliable boiler operation. If the level is too high, water can flow into the superheater with droplets carried into the turbine. This will leave deposits in the superheater and turbine, and in the extreme, cause superheater tube failure. Consequences of low level of water are even more severe. An insufficient head of water may cause a reduction in furnace circulation, cause tube overheating and failure. In order to maintain the level in the drum within the desired limits, feed-water control system is designed to regulate the flow of water to a drum type boiler to match

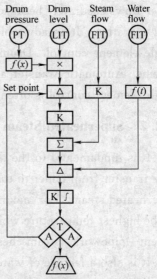

Fig. 6-1　Three-element cascade-feed forward control loop for feed-water

the flow of the steam out of the top of the drum. The control system will vary with the type and capacity of the boiler as well as with load characteristics.

On first sight, it would appear that flow could be controlled by a simple loop known as "single-element control system" to maintain drum level at a desired value, closing to mid-height of the drum. However, because the control signal satisfies the requirements of drum level only, excessive swell or shrink effects will result in unacceptable oscillations in the level following a quick load change.

The most widely used feed-water control system, especially in the utility industry, is the three-element feed-water control systerm shown in Fig. 6-1. It is a cascade-feed forward control loop. The outer loop employs proportional-plus-integral action to control drum water level. The inner loop employs proportional-plus-integral action to match the feed flow to the steam flow, the output from the outer loop acting as a trim on the steam flow signal. The advantages of this cascade arrangement are that the inner loop responds rapidly to load changes and the integral component in the outer loop permits a true desired value to be set.

During low load operation(0%~20%), it is difficult to obtain steam and water flows accurately because flow transmitters are usually calibrated for high load operation. It is advisable to transfer the feed-water control system to single element control. Drum level is the only variable used in the control scheme. Automatic transfer as a function of load between three-element and single-element control is often provided.

6.2.2　Superheated Steam Temperature Control

It is fundamental to the thermodynamics of power generation that the energy transfer from boiler to turbine is directly related to the temperature of the superheated steam. For maximum efficiency, therefore, the steam is delivered at the highest temperature which can be tolerated by the mechanical plant component—pipework, steam chests, valves, turbine blades, etc.

It is also a feature of water-tube boiler design that the temperature of the superheated steam increases approximately linearly with the boiler heat rate is increased. The aim of the boiler designer is to achieve the design steam temperature at a lower load level than full load, ideally at around 70%;at loads above this, the temperature is limited by attemperation. Besides boiler load variation, other operating variables, such as slag or ash accumulation on heat transfer surfaces, feed-water temperature, excess air, the type of fuel, etc. , also affect steam temperature in drum-type boiler. On the large boilers in service, the universal method of attemperating the superheated steam is to add water in the form of a fine spray. The saturated steam leaving the drum is subjected to several stages of superheating before it is delivered to the turbine.

After the first stage, the steam is directed along pipes external to the furnace where the spraywater is injected, and then to further banks of superheater tubes. The temperature of the steam leaving the final stage of superheating may therefore be controlled by regulating the flow of spraywater. To prolong the life of critical mechanical components of both boiler and turbine, fluctuations in steam temperature must be minimized. Spraywater flow must therefore be controlled automatically to maintain steam temperatures within very close limits.

Obviously, the primary controlled condition is the temperature of the steam leaving the final superheater stage. But the natural lag between a change in spraywater flow and the resultant change in this temperature is several minutes. So, if a simple loop were employed to control spraywater flow, using this temperature as the measured value, the response would be very sluggish and deviations following a load change would be unacceptable. It is standard practice, therefore, to arrange this control system as a cascade as shown in Fig. 6-2. This inner loop regulates the spraywater to control the temperature of the steam measured after it leaves the attemperator; this outer loop regulates the setpoint of the inner loop to control the final steam temperature.

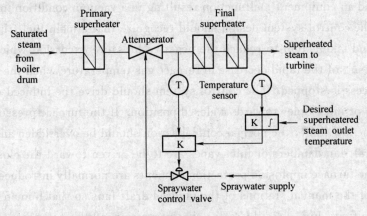

Fig. 6-2 Superheated system temperature control

On most systems found in practice, the inner loop regulates the spraywater control valve directly. However, on some boilers, the third control loop has been added to the cascade; this regulates the spray valve, using the actual spraywater flow as the measured value, the setpoint being provided by the attemperator temperature control loop. The effect of this third, innermost loop is to counteract fluctuations in the pressure of the spraywater supply. (The provision of an inner "flow loop" is dependent on suitable pipework geometry;

a simpler alternative is to derive a feedforward signal from the pressure drop across the feed regulating valves.)

6.2.3 Furnace Draft Control

The induced draft fan control portion of the system maintains flue gas side furnace pressure at a desired set point and provides furnace overpressure and implosion protection.

Overpressurization may create a major disturbance in the furnace resulting in partial or complete loss of flame. If fuel flow is not stopped immediately, furnace explosion may result. Typical system protection is to initiate a unit load runback on high furnace pressure until the induced draft (ID) fans can maintain the desired furnace pressure. If the furnace pressure exceeds the high limit for a predetermined time period, a boiler trip is desirable.

Furnace implosion is the result of a combination of a unit trip (flame collapse) and an equipment malfunction resulting in a vacuum condition in the furnace. The control system design should recognize that a main fuel trip has occurred and take action to reduce the negative pressure excursion which occurs as the result of the rapid decrease in furnace gas temperature when the combustion process is stopped. The control system should drive the induced draft fan dampers or inlet vanes towards a closed position. If the furnace pressure drops below the low limit, the normal control action should be overridden and the induced draft fan dampers or inlet vanes are to be driven toward the closed position. The furnace implosion protection elements are normally introduced downstream of the manual stations of the induced draft fans so that human action is not permitted. Fig. 6-3 illustrates the integration of the furnace draft overpressure protection and furnace implosion protection systems.

6.2.4 Combustion Control System

A combustion control system regulates the fuel and air input, or firing rate, to the furnace in response to a load index. The demand for firing rate is, therefore, a demand for energy input into the system to match a withdrawal of energy at some point in the cycle. For boiler operation and control systems, variations in the boiler outlet pressure are often used as an index of an unbalance between fuel-energy input and energy withdrawal in the output steam.

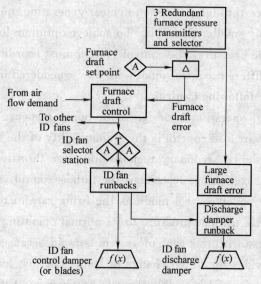

Fig. 6-3 Furnace draft control

A great variety of combustion control systems have been developed over the years to fit the needs of particular applications. Load demands, operating philosophy, plant layout, and types of firing must be considered.

6.2.5 Unit Load Control

The overall control of the electrical power delivered by a boiler or turbine-generator unit to the grid is a matter of maintaining a balance between the thermal power, produced by the boiler in the form of superheated steam at high pressure, and the mechanical power developed by the turbine from the steam delivered to it. A measure of the balance between the boiler load and the turbine load is therefore the constancy of the steam pressure at the inlet to the governor valves; if the turbine is demanding steam at a rate in excess of that being produced by the boiler, the steam pressure will decrease, and vice versa. Fundamental to all unit load control systems, therefore, is the control of the steam pressure at the inlet to the governor valves. However, if there is an imbalance between the boiler and the turbine loads, the steam pressure changes steadily(not abruptly)because the boiler has a thermal capacity, a proportion of the thermal energy is stored. For a large modern drum boiler, a change in demand equal to full-load would cause the pressure to fall by 10% in about 12 seconds. The once-through boilers on nuclear generating units have stored energies considerably smaller than this. To achieve optimum load response while maintaining stable pressure, the control system must coordinate the boiler and turbine. Three different control modes are now considered in detail.

6.2.5.1   Boiler-following Control

This mode of operation is designed for boiler response to follow turbine response. Megawatt load control is the responsibility of the turbine-generator. The boiler is assigned secondary responsibility for throttle pressure control. The demand for a load change repositions the turbine control valves. Following a load change, the boiler control modifies the firing rate to reach the new load level and to restore throttle pressure to its normal operating value.

Load response with this type of system is rapid because the stored energy in the boiler provides the initial change in load. The fast load response is obtained at the expense of less stable throttle pressure control. A boiler-following control system is illustrated in Fig. 6-4.

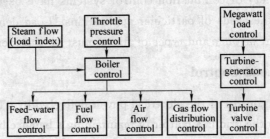

Fig. 6-4   Boiler-following control system

6.2.5.2   Turbine-following Control

In this operating mode, turbine response follows boiler response. Megawatt load control is the responsibility of the boiler while the turbine-generator is assigned secondary responsibility for throttle pressure control. With increasing load demand, the boiler control increases the firing rate which, in turn, raises throttle pressure. To maintain a constant throttle pressure, the turbine control valves open, increasing megawatt output. When a decrease in load is demanded, this process is reversed.

Load response with this type of system is rather slow because the turbine-generator must wait for the boiler to change its energy output before repositioning the turbine control valves to change load. However, this mode of operation will provide minimal steam pressure and temperature fluctuation during load change. A conventional turbine-following control system is shown in Fig. 6-5.

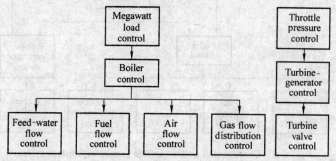

Fig. 6-5 Turbine-following control system

6.2.5.3 Coordinated Boiler-turbine Control

While both the above systems can provide satisfactory control, each has inherent disadvantages and neither fully exploits the capabilities of both the-boiler and turbine-generator. The turbine-following and boiler-following systems may be combined into a coordinated control system giving the advantages of both systems and minimizing the disadvantages. The coordinated boiler turbine-generator control system is shown in Fig. 6-6. Megawatt load control and throttle pressure control are the responsibility of both the boiler and the turbine-generator.

Because the boiler is not capable of producing rapid changes in steam generation at constant pressure, the turbine is used to provide initial load response. When a change in load is demanded, the throttle pressure set point is modified using megawatt error(the difference between the actual load and the load demand), and the turbine control valves respond to the change in set point to give the new load level quickly. As the boiler modifies the firing rate to reach the new load and restore throttle pressure, the throttle pressure returns to its normal value. The result is a fast and efficient production of electric power through proper coordination of the boiler and turbine-generator. The response is much faster than the turbine-following system, shown in Fig. 6-6.

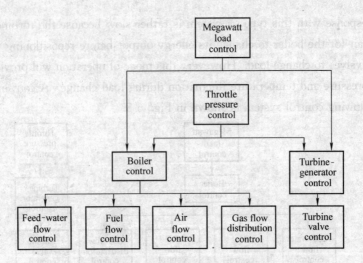

Fig. 6-6 Coordinated boiler turbine-generator control system

However, it is not as fast as the boiler-following system because the effect of megawatt error is limited to maintain a balance between boiler response and stability. Wider limits would provide more rapid response while narrower limits would provide more stabillty.

6.3 Integrated Operation from Central Control Room

Fig. 6-7 Integrated central control room

A power plant operation system for operating power plant equipment at a plant worksite through a central control room, and a network, comprising: an operation terminal positioned in the worksite for generating a request signal to operate the plant equipment at the plant worksite, the request signal including information concerning on-site operation at the worksite; a plurality of wireless transceivers located at appropriate points at the plant worksite for carrying out wireless communication between the operation terminal and a nearer one of the transceivers to receive the request signal generated by the operation terminal, the wireless transceivers being operatively connected to the network for transmitting the received request signal to the central control room; and a control device connected to the network for carrying out the operation of the plant equipment according to the request signal transmitted from the operation terminal through the network, wherein when a tag for prohibiting the operation of the plant equipment is set or canceled by the request signal generated by the operation terminal, information concerning the setting or cancellation of the tag is transmitted to the central control room and is displayed and output by a display device and a sound device.

Operators in plants with automated control systems work mainly in a central control room(Fig. 6-7) and usually are called control room operators or control room operator trainees or assistants. In older plants, the controls for the equipment are not centralized, and switchboard operators control the flow of electricity from a central point, whereas auxiliary equipment operators work throughout the plant, operating and monitoring valves, switches, and gauges (Fig. 6-8).

Boiler Operator Jeff Craigie sits in the Boiler Room and monitors flows, temperatures and pressures of the boilers and feed-water system. Photo by Ryan Solomon.

Fig. 6-8 Boiler control room

Power plant operators control and monitor boilers, turbines, generators, and auxiliary equipment in power-generating plants. Operators distribute power demands among generators, combine the current from several generators, and monitor instruments to maintain voltage and regulate electricity flows from the plant. When power requirements change, these workers start or stop generators and connect or disconnect them from circuits. They often use computers to keep records of switching operations and loads on generators, lines, and transformers. Operators may also use computers to prepare reports of unusual incidents, malfunctioning equipment, or maintenance performed during their shift.

Because electricity is provided around the clock, operators, distributors, and dispatchers usually work one of three daily eight-hour shifts or one of two twelve-hour shifts on a rotating basis. Shift assignments may change periodically, so all operators can share duty on less desirable shifts. Work on rotating shifts can be stressful and fatiguing, because of the constant change in living and sleeping patterns. Operators, distributors, and dispatchers who work in control rooms generally sit or stand at a control station. This work is not physically strenuous but requires constant attention. Operators who work outside the control room may be exposed to danger from electric shock, falls, and burns.

Extensive Reading

Samples of Job Opportunities

Operations Shift Technician Power Station

Employment type	Permanent
Location	Hampshire, Southampton
Industry sector	Civil
Start date	ASAP
Salary/rate	£33,000~38,000
Reference	0708-100
Date advertised	Yesterday ~18 : 05

Description

Operations Shift Technicians Power Station

Southampton, Hampshire

£ 33~38 k＋Overtime＋Relocation＋Bonus＋Pension＋Health

A brand new State of the Art CCGT 1,000 MW Power Station, in Southampton, Hampshire, is embarking on a substantial recruitment drive for Operations or Production Shift Technicians. These roles would ideally suit experienced Technicians from the Power, Chemical, Oil & Gas, Armed Forces (Army or Navy) or similar sectors. Your strengths are likely to lie in Mechanical, Electrical or Controls and Instrumentation.

You will be involved in the safe and efficient production of Power, and will support the Shift Team Leaders, to ensure that all equipment operates correctly and efficiently. An understanding of the Power Generation sector would be a definite advantage. Typical equipment on site includes large rotating machinery, Gas Turbines, Steam Turbines, Boilers and associated auxiliary plant equipment. The roles will run on an eight-hour shift, but for the first year the site will be in the commissioning stage, so you will work normal days.

Typically someone from a Production/Operations/Maintenance background, with Process experience, would work well in a role such as this. Ex Royal Navy / Army candidates would also be well suited. A relevant Engineering qualification is also important.

The successful candidate will receive a highly competitive salary in the region of £33~38 k along with a super benefits packaging including Overtime, Company Bonus Scheme (up to 15%), Pension Scheme, Private Healthcare and 24 days holiday (rising to 27 days). A generous relocation package is also available to candidates currently outside of the area.

To apply for this position please forward your CV to Darren Simmons at ASTUTE Technical Recruitment Ltd. by email Darren@astutetechnical.co.uk or call 02 392 658 210 to request any further information.

ASTUTE Technical Recruitment is a specialist in the Power and Energy sectors and has a number of opportunities throughout the UK and overseas. Please do call us to discuss your requirements in greater detail.

Please fill in the attached application form and send it together with your resume to mt@carrier. utc. com. Phone, fax or mail will not be received.

CARRIER CHINA OPERATIONS MANAGEMENT TRAINEE PROGRAM APPLICATION FORM

This application form, if answered carefully and completely, will provide the person interested in associating with Carrier China Operations an opportunity to present his or her complete background and history. This will enable the person to derive the greatest benefit from interview and as a part of out personal records.

Please print clearly in english/chinese to answer all questions.

1. Personal Data

English name		Chinese name		I. D. No.	
Nationality		Birthday		Available date	
Tel. No. (Home)		Office Telephone		BP, Mobile phone	
Home address(in Chinese)					
Post code		Contact person		Expected salary	

2. Family Members (in Chinese)

Relation	Name	Sex	Age	Job Title	Name, Address of Company/Dept	Tel.

3. Education Status

Type of School	Name and Address of School/University	Subject	From _ To _	Certificate
Secondary school				
College/university				
Scholarship obtained				
Social experience				
Other training courses				

4. Language Ability

Indicate Foreign Languages Capability Indicate"X"in Proper Columns (E—Excellent, G—Good, F—Fair)	Speak			Read			Write		
	E	G	F	E	G	F	E	G	F
First foreign language									
Second foreign language									
Other languages or dialects									

5. Other Skills

Computer skills	

6. Internship/Work Exprience

Employers	Duration	Job Title	Job Responsibilities	Reference(name, title&contact)

7. Please describe your personal weakness and strengths (Less than 500 words).

8. What is your career goal in short-term and long term (Less than 500 words).

9. What is your motivation in applying for?

10. Please list your personal unique selling point, quoting a few examples as reference. (Less than 500 words)

11. Statement

◆ I certify that the statements made in this application are true and correct.

◆ I accept that any false/inaccurate information or statement made by me will result in the immediate termination of my employment with this company.

◆ I also authorize any investigation of the above information for purposes of verification.

◆ I consent to take any pre-employment physical examination required by the Company and such future physical examinations as may be required by the company.

Writing about English Resume

（1）姓名，地址，联系方式，例如电话或者电子邮箱等。一般姓名采用居中的方式，其他的则居左就可以了。如下：

Name

Address

Phone No. Home

Cell phone No.

Email Add.

（2）objective（求职意向）。这一栏最重要，很多公司主要看这一栏的内容是否与他们所要求的一致或者接近。例如：

OBJECTIVE：

A sales management or business development position where my strategic and consultative selling, cross-cultural relationship building, team facilitation, business management，organizational insight，and advanced technical skills will be continually challenged. I aspire to senior management responsibility and seek a company that embraces growth and change, where compensation is performance-based and increased levels of responsibility offered those with demonstrated potential. （销售经理职位或者和企业发展有关的职位，可以使我的战略头脑、销售能力、建立跨文化关系的能力、团队能力、商务管理能力、组织能力和先进的技术能力都能够进一步的发挥和锻炼。……）

另外要注意的是，如果工作经验很多，也没有必要完全列举出来，可以挑几项自己感觉最得意的或者对自己提升最大的来写。

（3）Summary（个人简介）。这是展现自己能力的一个好机会，既要赞美自己，又不能使对方觉得在自夸。

（4）Experience（工作经验）。例如：

2005 —Present Company Sales Executive—Financial Services

Just started an exciting new position selling data integration solutions to the insurance and financial services vertical for Pervasive. Will try to update soon.

这是外国人普遍采用的表达方式。因为外国人从小就开始独立,他们可能从事过很多工作,这种方式即使是罗列很多也显得比较清晰,而且还把时间和当时的职位用一种比较明显的方式标注,也能突出重点。职位后面的那句话就是对你所担任的职位的简单描述。

(5)Education(教育背景)。一般从大学开始写起,包括时间、学校、专业、所获得的学位,以及 awards(所获的奖项),尤其是特殊奖项等。(注意:如果教育经历不多的话,一般教育和背景写在一起,但是如果教育背景或者奖项很突出的话,则可以另列一栏。)

以上是必写的内容。还有一些可以有选择性地写,比如 associations(参加的社团组织)。现在的公司对计算机或者外语能力都有一定的要求,所以还可以写自己的 **computer background**(计算机能力)和 **language skills**(外语能力),最后还可以写一栏 **personal profile**(个人评价),比如:

A dynamic, articulate, talented leader, manager and sales professional who inspires confidence and respect, grasps ideas and concepts quickly, is adept at organizing complex projects, recognizes or creates solutions to problems, believes in setting and achieving goals, and possesses the integrity and commitment to high quality performance that produces outstanding results of lasting value.

除此之外,还可以加上一些个人情况,例如婚姻情况、身体状况及业余爱好等等。

New Words and Expressions

actuator *n.*	执行器,执行机构
ancillary *a.*	辅助的
attemperator *n.*	保温器
cascade *n.*	联结,串联
cascade-feedforward	串级一前馈
circuit-breaker	断路器
conductivity *n.*	传导率
coordinate *v.*	协调
damper *n.*	挡板,调节风门
dispatcher *n.*	调度员,调度程序,配电器

distributed control system	分散控制系统
disturbance n.	干扰，扰动
draft n.	通风，(炉膛及烟道)负压
excess air	过量空气
excitation n.	激发，激励
failure n.	破坏，故障
filter n.	滤波(器)
firing rate	燃烧率
furnace purge	炉膛吹扫
governor valve	调节阀
heat rate	热耗(率)，热容量
inlet vane	进口叶片
lag n.	滞后，迟延，惯性
once-through boiler	直流锅炉
overheating	过热，超温
primary air fan	一次风机
proportional controller	比例控制器
sensor n.	传感器
set point	设定值
shrink v.	变小，收缩
shutdown n.	停机，停炉，停运
single-element	单冲量
smart a.	灵敏的
start up	启动
swell v.	膨胀，隆起
throttle pressure	(汽轮机)入口压力
transformer n.	变压器
trip n.	跳闸
temperature difference	温差
drive n.	驱动器
retain v.	保留
sensitivity n.	灵敏度

Part Ⅶ

Unit Operation

● 中文概要

1. 单元机组启机、投负荷的步骤与注意事项
2. 单元机组减负荷、停机的步骤与注意事项

Effective operation of power plant equipment such as boiler and turbine is critical to maintaining unit efficiency, reliability and availability. The procedures used to run power plant equipment vary widely depending upon the type of unit. There are, however, a set of relatively common fundamental operating guidelines which safeguard personnel and optimize unit performance and reliability. The following material covers the fundamentals of unit operation.

7.1 Unit Operation—Start up and Loading

7.1.1 Pre-start Checking

In recent years, not only has the complexity of plant increased but the cost penalties incurred by a late return to service have also risen steeply, as a result, there has been a general tendency towards the adoption of a formal system of pre-start checking. Pre-start checking of the power station equipment serves two purposes: it familiarizes the operator with the equipment, and it verifies the condition of the equipment.

7. 1. 2 Boiler Conditions

7. 1. 2. 1 Filling and Hydraulic Testing

Hydraulic tests on boilers are done for two main reasons.

(1) To satisfy the boiler insurer's representative at agreed intervals following major refurbishment or overhaul that the boiler is safe for continued operation. The pressure to which the boiler is raised may exceed the normal operating pressure (referred to as the maximum permissible working pressure, MPWP) and is called an overpressure test.

(2) As a means of testing for leaks, either before a major overhaul or after minor tube repairs have been effected. Here, the hydraulic test pressure never exceeds the MPWP and is often only a fraction of it, as the aim is to check that no leaks exist rather than to subject any minor repairs to a pressure that will prove their ability to withstand normal operation, a requirement that is fulfilled just as adequately by some form of non-destructive testing, e. g. ultrasonic testing.

The basic operating requirements for hydraulic testing are quite straightforward and are set out below.

(1) The quality of the water used for the test should be as high as practicable. This is particularly important where austenitic steels are present in the boiler pressure parts, as any appreciable amounts of chlorides present in the water can induce the stress-corrosion cracking of this steel. The requirement is satisfied by the specification for modem water treatment plants, i. e. a conductivity not exceeding 10 μs/m at the plant outlet.

(2)The temperature of the water must be greater than 7 ℃ at all times in order to eliminate any possibility of freezing.

(3)Drum differentials must never be exceeded.

(4)No air should be trapped in the boiler pressure parts during the hydrostatic test. As the boiler is being filled, each available vent should be open until water appears.

Finally, if all the above considerations have been acted upon and no major boiler leaks of any description are present, it should be possible to maintain the test pressure for a period with the boiler feed pump isolated from the boiler, or at least using a percentage of the discharge by-pass valve flow only under which conditions the potential energy stored in the boiler pressure parts is the minimum practicable and the personal safety of the inspection party is assured so far as is possible.

The normal tilling of the boiler to working level can be accomplished very rapidly provided that drum differentials allow. Examples are on record where a 500 MW boiler was ready for tiring within the hour, the main limitations being the replenishment of the deaerator and the rapid removal of the large quantities of air displaced from the boiler.

7.1.2.2 Pressure Raising

Drum differentials are most likely to be exceeded when filling a hot drum with cool water or during pressure raising or forced-cooling operations. Modern drums extend to 36 m or more in length and have wall thicknesses of, typically, 100 mm. Such massive structures can be seriously damaged by repeated metal yielding (leading to fatigue cracking) brought about by thermal stresses set up by differential temperature changes occurring either across drum walls (inner-to-outer surfaces), across drum top-to-bottom surfaces or along the length of the drum.

To minimize thermal stressing during start up or shutdown, it is necessary to limit and control the temperature gradients occurring both across the walls and between drum top and bottom surfaces, these being related such that if one is high, the other must be kept low, and vice versa. The whole scenario is also dependent on the internal operating pressure.

Top-to-bottom differences can be effectively controlled on some cases by the use of drum spray, especially during forced-cooling activities when no steam is being drawn through the superheaters and so no danger of water carryover can be present; conversely, the use of drum spray under light-up conditions is often restricted whilst boiler steamside drains are open.

A cold furnace is preferably fired by the use of oil burners because the heat input can be better controlled than when using PF, and because the short, localized radiant oil flame is much better suited to initial pressure raising than the slower-burning PF flame, which can result in the overheating of superheater elements until a good steam flow is established through them. Every effort must be made to obtain good combustion, especially whilst the furnace is cold, and oil burners should be used in combinations that give the best possible mutual support. Faulty or smoky burners should not be used. Adequate control over initial combustion from the control room is very difficult and it is always beneficial to provide a person locally to monitor conditions. Certain oil burner selections may also be necessary in order to keep the heat away from any vulnerable radiant superheater surfaces located in the furnace, unless they are equipped with sufficient and reliable metal-temperature thermocouples to monitor their condition effectively.

Pressure raising is usually limited to a rate that gives a $50\sim80\,°C/h$ change in drum saturated-steam temperature. This allows the full boiler pressure to be achieved from cold in 5 hours on a 160 bar boiler, always provided that drum differential and superheater/reheater metal-temperature limits are not exceeded. During pressure rising, the reheater is particularly vulnerable, as it sees no steam flow at all until the turbine is running. For this reason, it is usual to bypass as much flue gas as possible away from the tube banks.

Superheater circuit drainage varies to suit the needs of the particular installation but conforms to the following principles. Intermediate and boiler final-drains usually perform different functions. The former are installed to allow the removal of condensate which can collect in large quantities in the inlet headers to intermediate superheater stages and, if not removed, can prevent steam flow through some, or all, of the following stages, causing overheating. The danger is particularly acute in the case of a steam furnace-division wall. Intermediate drains should only normally be operated sufficiently to remove the condensate; this may entail intermittent operation, or the use of condensate in drain line detection equipment, such as the Hydratect system.

Final superheater drains perform a different, or at least, an additional function, they promote sufficient steam flow through the superheater as a whole to keep the various sections "cool". In consequence, the drainage applied, whilst often varying with the type of startup, is invariably continuous until steam flow is transferred to the turbine steam-lead drains or to the turbine itself.

7. 1. 2. 3 Purging

Considerable attention has been given to the prevention of furnace explosions, especially on units burning fuel in suspension. Most furnace explosions occur during startup and low load periods. Whenever the possibility exists for the accumulation of combustible gases or combustible dust in any part of the unit no attempt should be made to light the burners until the unit has been thoroughly purged. The accepted practice on multiple burner units is to purge with 25% of full load rated air flow for five minutes.

7. 1. 3 Turbine Considerations

7. 1. 3. 1 Preparation

Pre-start activities vary with machines and ancillary systems. but the following general principles still apply.

(1)Commission turbine lubricating oil system. Paying particular attention to the need to raise the oil temperature to normal prior to run up. Barring speeds vary between machines, the jacking oil pumps may have to run continuously thereafter until the turbine run-up is in progress. This activity is usually done in conjunction with the generator preparation.

(2)Set turbine drains systems.

(3)Charge condensers with circulating water and establish a starting flow.

(4)Commission the pumps of any fire-resistant fluid system installed for turbine valve control, raising the fluid temperature to normal.

(5)Set and prove the turbine trip gear. Exercising steam valves according to instructions. Limitations in valve rift may apply while valve seats are cold.

(6) Commission or set auxiliary systems, e. g. condenser extraction pumps, gland-sealing and flange heating systems and vacuum-raising plant.

(7)Commission turbine supervisory equipment.

(8)Ensure that the fire protection systems are correctly set. Following a major outage, it is usual to initiate the deluge systems to ensure that all nozzles are in place and are correctly positioned and operating.

7.1.3.2　Thermal Constraints

1. Basic Principles

A steam turbine is primarily designed to carry its load at rated speed and under specified steam inlet conditions. It may be safely assumed, by and large, that it will do this once stable conditions have been achieved. Such conditions include the establishment of normal temperature gradients from inlet to outlet and the free development of all thermal expansions. If it were possible to put the machine very quickly into this condition, then the most rapid starts would be possible and desirable. Unfortunately, that situation is only approached when restarting a very hot machine after the briefest of shutdowns, such as might occur, for example, after an inadvertent trip from a high load with an immediate restart. All other turbine starts fall short of this ideal to a greater or lesser extent.

To limit stresses in thick metal sections, the starting process resolves fundamentally into a controlled heating exercise of main steam leads, steam chests and turbine components and, as the heating steam also drives the turbine, it follows that the rate-of-rise of turbine speed and load is also controlled (restricted) by the heating process to a degree dependent on the temperature of the metal parts. The object, in starting, is to control the admission of steam passing into steam heads, chests and turbine casings to effect a run-up in the minimum time consistent with keeping metal stresses within acceptable limits. Experience and research have shown that with the thickest of metal sections currently in use, thermal stresses will be acceptable if the rate-of-change of surface metal temperatures are below $150\sim200$ °C/h, assuming that the sections are heated from one side only. For the more complex, non-symmetrical sections the acceptable rate falls and a general working limit of 120 °C/h(2 °C/min)is often specified and can be regarded as typical. Not so long ago some turbine manufacturers, in setting down operating instructions for their plant, specified only acceptable steam inlet conditions, run-up times and subsequent loading rates for a range of pre-start HP and IP turbine metal-temperatures, arguing that providing these were adhered to heating rates it would be automatically acceptable. With the general introduction of Visual Display Unit (VDU) displays, it had been found much more information can be assimilated by the operator and a series of programmes showing actual rates-of-rise of metal-temperatures in steam chests and turbine components can be provided.

when steam is applied to a metal section, the steam quality should be such that, any necessary(or inevitable)throttling, its temperature will be above that of the metal surface. The temperature difference should be enough to give a reasonable heating rate, but not enough to induce excessive surface stresses. Heat transfer is much higher under saturated steam conditions than under superheat and the former must be avoided if at all possible, especially in places where drainage is poor or non-existent. On earlier 500 MW turbines the steam chests were often problematic; later designs have provision for drainage and preheating can be achieved, prior to turbine run-up, by closing the governing valves and partly opening the emergency stop valves.

2. Main Steam Leads and Chest

Before opening boiler stop valves (BSV), the final steam temperature should be adjusted such that after throttling to atmospheric pressure, it will match the steam lead metal-temperature. If this is not measured directly, and this is by no means uncommon, it can be inferred either from steam chest metal-temperature readings or from those displayed on steam lead steam-temperature indicators. These will be a good match of metal temperature provided that the steam leads have been "boxed in" during the shutdown period, with drain valves left closed. If the boiler is completely depressurized initially and the steam leads are below 100 ℃, they may be warmed through along with the boiler by firing with BSVs open.

HP steam chests are particularly vulnerable to overstressing and in recent years have often been extensively equipped with through-wall differential metal-temperature monitoring. During cold or warm starts, the chest is normally colder than the steam and a heating transient occurs which can give rise to sufficient stress to cause thermal fatigue damage. Heating transients are sometimes called up-shock events; conversely, chilling or cooling transients give rise to down-shock. Chilling occurs when the steam temperature falls below the metal temperature, the contraction of the inner metal—a condition commonly referred to in the past as corrosion fatigue cracking. Another source of chilling is water leaking past BSVs during boiler hydraulic testing.

3. Cold Starts

Cold starts are defined as cold if steam chest and/or turbine metal-temperatures are below 75 ℃. Traditionally, in these cases, the method used has been to raise boiler pressure to a value at which the turbine glands can be sealed. This is often around 30 bar but may surprisingly be higher. The steam leads are warmed through at the same time and fully pressurized when their temperature allows, vacuum-raising plant then being commissioned and the turbine glands sealed. Vacuum is raised to a level that allows the machine to be rolled on steam; this need not be high at first, but must be increased to normal before the turbine speed is raised above 2,000 r/min. Run-up times vary between machines but can be as long as two hours and may involve "holds" in speed, often below 1,000 r/min in order to allow a measure of heating and expansion to occur.

Another method that has been tried with one make of machine involves the pre-warming of the HP and, to a lesser extent, the IP turbine prior to run-up. This is achieved by closing the IP emergency stop and intercept valves and introducing steam into the chests, HP turbine and reheater steam circuit as soon as the glands can be sealed and a small vacuum raised. The pressure is allowed to rise slowly to about 7 bar in two hours and is then held at that value for a further two hours. The machine may roll off barfing and run at a few hundred revolutions per minute. A small flow of heating steam passes into the IP turbine via the shaft cooling line (this being provided to seal and cool the stagnant central section of the double-flow IP cylinder and rotor with relatively cold HP exhaust(cold reheat)steam at all times). At the end of the process, HP and IP turbine metal-temperatures have risen to about 240 ℃, allowing the machine to be run up to speed and loaded to the warm-start curves, resulting in a small reduction in the overall time taken to reach full-load.

4. Warm Starts

Warm starts are defined as warm when the HP turbine valve chest and/or turbine metal-temperatures are between 75 ℃ and 300 ℃. In practice, these starts can be more troublesome than cold or hot starts as a result of complications arising with turbine differential expansions. Run-up times may be quoted to suit turbine conditions but in practice may be dictated by the requirement to warm the steam chests to within 20 ℃ of saturated steam temperature before they are pressurized. Steam conditions at turbine stop valves should be adjusted during the vacuum-raising process such that, after throttling to about 4 bar (the initial inlet-stage pressure), they match the HP turbine inner-casing temperature. Once on-load, the machine is loaded to the warm-start curves.

5. Hot Starts

Hot starts are defined as hot when the HP turbine valve chest and/or inlet metal-temperatures are above 300 ℃. With such starts, provided that the boiler pressure is held down to a sensible level, saturation heating is impossible. Steam conditions should again be such that, after throttling to 4 bar, they match the HP inner casing temperature. Run-up times range from less than 5 minutes for the hottest conditions to 10 minutes. If the turbine inlet metal-temperature is much in excess of 400 ℃, it is unlikely that the inner casing temperature will be matched until the machine is on-load and an initial block load is applied. Such a load would, typically, be 10%～20% of rated full-load. Subsequent load increases are to the hot-start loading curves.

7.2 Unit Operation—De-Loading and Shutdown

Not unexpectedly, the reason for the unit shutdown will influence the deloading procedure to be adopted. For example, if the shutdown is for two-shifting purposes, it is important not only to maintain the highest possible turbine metal-temperature prior to shutdown, but also to agree on a target boiler pressure at which to come off load. High turbine metal-temperatures allow rapid subsequent reloading of the turbine, as the temperature loss due to natural off-loads cooling will be at a minimum. A solution may be to reduce load initially to about half-load at a rate to suit system separations requirements, taking out of service as much of the milling plant as possible. The target boiler pressure chosen at which to come off load is such as to allow the desired start-up steam temperature to be achieved without risking an excessively high boiler pressure during lightup.

During this period opportunity is taken to adjust other unit conditions, such activities may include:

(1) The completion of any previously-initiated air heater sootblowing sequence.

(2) The cooling of the remaining in-service mills to avoid any possibility of internal coal deposits from firing during the shutdown period. It is quite common to limit the shutdown internal mill air temperature to 50 ℃ for this reason.

(3) The effective isolation, whatever this implies, of the superheater and reheater desuperheat spray systems.

(4) The transfer of the boiler feed-water requirements from the turbine-driven feed pump to the standby, motor-driven unit.

(5) The transfer of the unit electrical supplies from the unit transformer to the station switchboard.

Once the necessary unit conditions have been achieved and permission to shutdown has been granted, oil burners are commissioned (if not already in use) and shutdown procedures are simultaneously implemented on the remaining mills. As soon as the coal flames are extinguished, the oil burners are tripped (usually via the ignition trip button to check its operation) and the unit load is reduced quickly to zero. Generator motoring conditions are proven and the main circuit-breaker is opened as soon as the active and reactive loadings on the generator have been readjusted to zero. The turbine steam valves must not be tripped-closed to shut down the machine until the generator excitation control has been placed on "manual" and reduced. Once the steam valves have been tripped-closed, all that remains to be done is to check that the standby lubricating oil pump starts automatically(as the output from the shaft-driven oil pump falls with speed)and that bearing oil pressure is maintained, also that the turbine speed is falling at the expected rate.

Meanwhile, on the boiler, once ignition is tripped and while the stipulated furnace purge is proceeding, it is essential to conduct checks(locally, if necessary)to ensure that all oil burner flames are out and that oil is not leaking into the furnace. Boiler fans can now be shut down and gas-side dampers tightly closed to minimize the loss of heat convection and pressure decay. Thereafter, boiler stop valves can be closed and steam-leads depressurized, condenser CW flows curtailed and CW pumps shutdown.

Other shutdown actions may include:

(1)The isolation of all condensate make-up supplies to the condenser, as soon as possible and in any event before vacuum is broken to reduce oxygen levels in the system to a minimum.

(2)The maintenance of lubricating and seal-oil temperatures and hydrogen gas temperatures as appropriate.

(3)The topping-up of the boiler drum to a level that obviates the need to restart the feed pump during the shutdown period. The level is arrived at by experience, but is seldom less than the maximum reading displayed on the drum wide-range level indicator.

Extensive Reading

科技论文英文摘要的书写规范

文摘是原始文献的代表。它提供了原始文献的信息内容,但不能代替原始文献(即一次文献),因为其内容已大大简化。

文摘本身给读者一个信息,即该篇文献所包含的主要概念和讨论的主要问题。它能够帮助科技人员决定这篇文献是否对自己的工作有用。

《美国工程索引》(The Engineering Index)是世界最有名也是最大的检索

刊物之一。每月出版一期，报道世界工程文献文摘 1,3000～1,4000 条，每期有刊附的主题索引与作者索引，每年还另出版年卷本和年度索引，年度索引中还增加了作者单位索引。出版形式有印刷版（期刊形式）、电子版（磁带）及缩微胶片，曾出版过检索卡片，但已于 1975 年停止发行。

1. 文摘的种类（Type of Abstracts）

按美国工程信息公司编辑部（EI 编辑部）的分类，文摘分为指示性文摘与信息性文摘或者两者结合的文摘。

信息性文摘（Information Abstracts）一般包括了原始文献某些重要内容的梗概，主要由以下三部分组成。

（1）目的：主要说明作者写此文章的目的，或本文要解决的问题。

（2）过程及方法：说明作者主要工作过程及所用的方法，也包括众多的边界条件、使用的主要设备和仪器。

（3）结果：作者通过此工作过程最后得到的结果和结论以及作者所得结果和结论的应用范围和应用情况。

信息性文摘多用于科技期刊的文章，也用于会议论文及各种专题学术报告。一般情况下信息性文摘占有绝大部分比例。

指示性文摘（Indicated Abstracts）仅指出文献的综合内容，适用于综述性文献、图书介绍及编辑加工过的专著等。综述性文献最常见的情况是概括介绍某技术在某时期的综合发展情况，或某技术在目前的发展水平及未来展望等。总之，这种文献是综述情况而不是某个技术工艺、某产品或某设备的研究过程。

2. 文摘长度（Length of the Abstracts）

英文文摘长度一般不超过 150 个单词，不少于 100 个单词，少数情况下可以例外，视原文文献而定，但主题概念不得遗漏。据统计，如根据前述三部分写文摘一般都不会少于 100 个单词。另外，写、译或校文摘可不受原文文摘的约束。

一般缩短文摘方法如下。

（1）取消不必要的字句：如"It is reported..." "Extensive investigations show that..." "The author discusses..." "This paper is concerned with...".

（2）对物理单位及一些通用词可以适当进行简化。

（3）取消或减少背景情况（Background Information）。

（4）限制文摘只表示新情况、新内容，对过去的研究细节可以取消。

（5）语句简洁，突出重点。如"本文所谈的有关研究工作是对过去老工艺的一个极大的改进"切不可进入文摘。

（6）作者在文献中谈及的未来计划不纳入文摘。

(7)尽量简化一些措辞和重复的单元。如：

复杂	简化
at a high pressure of 2,000 Pa	at 2,000 Pa
at a temperature of 250 ℃ to 300 ℃	at 250～300 ℃
at a high temperature of 1,500 ℃	at 1,500 ℃
has been found to increase	increased

此外请注意,文摘第一句话切不可与题目(Title)重复。

例如,不用"WAVE FUNCTION FOR THE H CENTER IN LIF. A wave function for the H center in LiF is proposed assuming a linear combination of appropriate molecular orbits. The…",而用"WAVE FUNCTION FOR THE H CENTER IN LIF. A linear combination of appropriate molecular orbit is assumed. The…"。

3. 文体风格(Styles)

文摘句文体风格需注意以下几点。

(1)文摘叙述要简明,逻辑性要强。

(2)句子结构严谨完整,尽量用短句。

(3)技术术语尽量用工程领域的通用标准用语。

(4)用过去时态叙述作者工作,用现在时态叙述作者结论。

(5)尽量采用-ing 分词和-ed 分词作定语,少用关系代词 which ,who 等引导的定语从句。

(6)可用动词的情况尽量避免用动词的名词形式。如:用"Thickness of plastic sheets was measured",不用"Measurement of thickness of plastic sheet was made"。

(7)注意冠词用法,分清 a 是泛指,the 是专指。如:"Pressure is a function of temperature"不应写为"Pressure is a function of the temperature ","The refinery operates…"不应写为" Refinery operates…"。

(8)避免使用多个形容词或名词来修饰名词,可用预置短语分开或用连字符(Hyphen)断开名词词组,作为单位形容词(一个形容词)。

(9)不使用俚语或外来语表达概念,应用标准英语。

(10)尽量用主动语态代替被动语态。如"A exceeds B"优于"B is exceeded by A"。

(11)语言要简练,但不得使用电报语言。如:"Adsorption nitrobenzene on

copper chronite investigation"应为"Adsorption of nitrobenzene on copper chronite was investigated"。

(12)文词要朴实严谨,避免文学性描述手法。如:"Working against time on hot slag and spilled metal in condition of choking dust and blinding steam, are conditions no maker would choose for his machines to operate in. "

(13)句子结构匀称,动词应尽量靠近主语。例如:不用"The decolorazation in solutions of the pigment in dioxane, which were exposed to 10 hr of UV irradiation, was no longer irreversible",而用"When the pigment was dissolved in dioxane, decolorization was irreversible after 10 hr of UV irradiation"。

(14)文摘中涉及他人的工作或研究成果时,尽量列出其名字。

(15)文摘词语拼写,用英美拼法均可,但每篇中应保持一致。

(16)用重要的事实开头,尽量避免用辅助从句开头。例如:用"Power consumption of telephone switching systems was determined from data obtained experimentally",而不用"From data obtained experimentally, power consumption of telephone switching systems was determined"。

(17)英文题目开头第一个词不得用 the,and,an 和 a。

(18)题目中尽量少用缩略词,必要时亦需在括号中注明全称(尽管中文文献题目中常用英文缩略字或汉语拼音缩略字),特殊字符及希腊字母在题目中尽量不用或少用。

4. 文摘中的特殊字符(Special Characters)

特殊字符主要指各种数学符号及希腊字母,EI 对它们的录入有特殊的规定。在文摘中尽量少用特殊字符及数学表达式,因为它们的输入极为麻烦,而且易出错,影响文摘本身的准确性,应尽量取消或用文字表达。

5. 文摘造句

熟悉英文摘要的常用句型。尽管英文的句型种类繁多,但摘要的常用句型却很有限,而且形成了一定的规律,大体可归纳为如下几点。

(1)表示研究目的,常用在摘要之首。如:"In order to..." "This paper describes..." "The purpose of this study is..."。

(2)表示研究的对象与方法。如:"The curative effect/sensitivity/function of certain drug/kit/organ was observed/detected/studied..."。

(3)表示研究的结果。如:"The result showed/It proved/The authors found that..."。

(4)表示结论、观点或建议。如:"The authors suggest/conclude/consider

that..."。

文摘范例

75 t/h 循环流化床锅炉床温影响因素的试验

摘　要：在一台 75 t/h 循环流化床锅炉上进行了燃用不同煤种、不同负荷和不同一次风量对床温影响的试验。试验表明，煤挥发份含量较低时，床温沿炉膛高度逐渐降低，但返料温度明显升高；负荷提高，床温整体升高，但炉膛底部与中部的温差减小；一次风量增加，会导致烟气从密相区带走的热量大于燃烧放热而使床温降低。

关键词：循环流化床锅炉；返料器；床温；负荷；一次风；燃料特性

TEST STUDY ON FACTORS AFFECTING BED TEMPERATURE OF 75 t/h CFB BOILER

Abstract：A test study on influence of different coal sort, different load and different air flow rate upon the bed temperature was carried out on a 75 t/h circulating fluidized bed (CFB) boiler. The test shows that the bed temperature is gradually reduced along the height of furnace in case of lower volatile matter content in the coal sort, but the temperature of returned material is obviously enhanced; the bed temperature is entirely increased in the event of increasing the load, but the temperature difference between bottom and centre of the furnace being decreased; the heat quantity carried out by the flue gas from dense-phase region is greater than that released from combustion while increasing the primary air flow rate, thus making the bed temperature to be lowered.

Key words：CFB boiler; returned material's container; bed temperature; load; primary air; fuel property

New Words and Expressions

auxiliary	*a.*	辅助的
casing	*n.*	汽缸
constraint	*v.*	约束，强制
deluge system		溢流系统
emergency stop valve		危急遮断阀，主汽门

gland-sealing	汽封,轴封
hydraulic *a.*	水力的,水压的
inadvertent trip	误动作,乱跳闸
steam chest	(蒸汽室、汽轮机)进汽箱
stress corrosion	应力腐蚀
thermal fatigue	热(应力)疲劳
warm start	暖态启动,半热态启动
by and large	大体上
drainage *n.*	排水,疏水
flange *n.*	法兰
hot start	热态启动
hydrostatic *a.*	静水力学的
intercept valve	截止阀,截流阀
pre-start checking	启动前检查
steam lead	蒸汽导管,蒸汽管道
switchboard *n.*	配电盘,控制板
transfer *v.*	转让,转换
VDU	直观显示装置
yielding *a.*	屈服的,易弯的

Part VIII

Environmental Protection

●中文概要

1. 环境污染问题
2. 锅炉排气及控制
3. 除尘器种类及工作原理

8.1 Introduction

Protecting the environment and making use of natural resources are two of the most pressing demands in the present stage of social development.

Power engineering, which is the basis for development of all branches of industry, transport and agriculture, has the highest rates of progress and scale of production. Organic fuel burned at thermal power stations contains harmful impurities which are ejected into the environment as gaseous and solid components of combustion products and can adversely affect the atmosphere and water.

The control of the atmosphere at thermal power stations is mainly aimed at minimizing the discharge of toxic substances into the atmosphere. The best results in this respect have been achieved in decreasing the discharge of solid ash particles (the degree of ash collection at thermal power stations is now as high as 99.5 %). Contamination of the atmosphere with sulphur oxides can be prevented both by removing sulphur from the fuel and applying means for cleaning flue gases from sulphurous compounds. Ejections of nitrogen oxides and certain carcinogenic substances are diminished by properly organizing the combustion process in boiler furnaces. Only after all possible methods of reducing harmful effluents have been utilized, can measures be taken for the effective dispersion of residual harmful impurities in the atmosphere where they are diluted to concentrations which can do virtually no harm to both nature and mankind.

In contrast to thermal power stations which use organic fuels, atomic power stations produce electric energy by means of nuclear fission which has a low consumption of nuclear fuel. Therefore, harmful effluents from atomic power stations in the atmosphere are insignificant and mainly admixtures in the ventilation air. It should be kept in mind, however, that radioactive isotopes which form in nuclear reactors have a high toxicity and their effect on living organisms may be accumulative. For that reason, the problem of disposal, transport and storage of solid and liquid radioactive wastes at atomic power stations are extremely important.

Though thermal power stations are not among the worst contaminants of water basins, in terms of the scope and composition of their liquid wastes, their discharges into water basins can cause great harm if proper measures are not taken for water protection. Another serious problem is thermal contamination of water basins.

8.2　Boiler Emissions and Control

Boiler emissions vary depending on fuel type and environmental conditions. Boilers emissions include nitrogen oxide (NO_x), sulfur oxides (SO_x), particulate matter (PM), carbon monoxide (CO), and carbon dioxide (CO_2).

8. 2. 1　Nitrogen Oxides (NO_x)

The pollutant referred to as NO_x is a mixture of (mostly) nitric oxide (NO) and nitrogen dioxide (NO_2) in variable composition. NO_x is formed by three mechanisms: thermal NO_x, prompt NO_x, and fuel-bound NO_x. In industrial boilers, thermal and fuel-bound are the predominant NO_x formation mechanisms. Thermal NO_x, formed when nitrogen and oxygen in the combustion air combine in the flame, comprises the majority of NO_x formed during the combustion of gases and light oils. Fuel-bound NO_x is associated with oil fuels and forms when nitrogen in the fuel and oxygen in the combustion air react. The most significant factors influencing the level of NO_x emissions from a boiler are the flame temperature and the amount of nitrogen in the fuel. Other factors include excess air level and combustion air temperature.

8. 2. 2　Sulfur Oxides(SO_x)

Emissions of sulfur relate directly to the sulfur content of the fuel, and are not dependent on boiler size or burner design. Sulfur dioxide (SO_2) composes about 95% of the emitted sulfur and with the remaining 5% emitted as sulfur trioxide (SO_3). SO_x are pollutants because they react with water vapor and form sulfuric acid mist, which is extremely corrosive and damaging in its air, water and soil-borne forms. Boiler fuels containing sulfur are primarily coal, oil, and some types of waste.

8. 2. 3　Particulate Matter (PM)

PM emissions are largely dependent on the grade of boiler fuel, and consist of many different compounds, including nitrates, sulfates, carbons, oxides and other uncombusted fuel elements. PM levels from natural gas are significantly lower than those of oils, and distillate oils much lower than residual oils. For industrial and commercial boilers, the most effective method of PM control is use of higher-grade fuel, and ensuring proper burner setup, adjustment and maintenance.

8. 2. 4　Carbon Monoxide (CO)

CO forms during combustion when carbon in the fuel oxidizes incompletely, ending up as CO instead of CO_2. Older boilers generally have higher levels of CO than new equipment because older burner designs do not have CO controls. Poor burner design or firing conditions are responsible for high levels of

CO boiler emissions. Proper burner maintenance or equipment upgrades, or using an oxygen control package, can control CO emissions successfully.

8.2.5 Carbon Dioxide (CO_2)

While not considered as a regulated pollutant in the ordinary sense of directly affecting public health, emissions of carbon dioxide are of concern due to its contribution to global warming. Atmospheric warming occurs because solar radiation readily penetrates to the surface of the planet but infrared (thermal) radiation from the surface is absorbed by the CO_2 (and other polyatomic gases such as water vapor, methane, unburned hydrocarbons, refrigerants and volatile chemicals) in the atmosphere, with resultant increase in temperature of the atmosphere. The amount of CO_2 emitted is a function of both fuel carbon content and system efficiency. The fuel carbon content of natural gas is 34 lbs carbon/MMBtu; oil is 48 lbs carbon/MMBtu; and (ashfree) coal is 66 lbs carbon/MMBtu.

8.2.6 Boiler Emissions Control Options—NO_x

NO_x control has been the primary focus of emission control research and development in boilers. The following provides a description of the most prominent emission control approaches.

1. Combustion Process Emissions Control

Combustion control techniques are less costly than post-combustion control methods and are often used in industrial boilers for NO_x control. Control of combustion temperature has been the principal focus of combustion process control in boilers. Combustion control requires trade-off high temperatures favour complete burn up of the fuel and low residual hydrocarbons and CO, but promote NO_x formation. Lean combustion dilutes the combustion process and reduces combustion temperatures and NO_x formation, and allows a higher compression ratio or peak firing pressures resulting in higher efficiency. However, if the mixture is too lean, misfiring and incomplete combustion occurs, increasing CO and VOC emissions.

2. Flue Gas Recirculation (FGR)

FGR is the most effective technique for reducing NO_x emissions from industrial boilers with inputs below 100 MMBtu/hr. With FGR, a portion of exhaust gases of the relatively cool boiler re-enter the combustion process, reducing the flame temperature and associated thermal NO_x formation. It is the most popular and effective NO_x reduction method for fire-tube and water-tube boilers, and many applications can rely solely on FGR to meet environmental standards.

External FGR employs a fan to recirculate the flue gases into the flame, with external piping carrying the gases from the stack to the burner. A valve responding to boiler input controls the recirculation rate. Induced FGR relies on the combustion air fan for flue gas recirculation. A portion of the gases travel via ductwork or internally to the air fan, where they are premixed with combustion air and introduced into the flame through the burner. Induced FGR in newer designs uses an integral design that is relatively uncomplicated and reliable. The physical limit to NO_x reduction via FGR is 80% in natural gas-fired boilers and 25% for standard fuel oils.

3. Low Excess Air Firing (LEAF)

Excess air ensures complete combustion. However, excess air levels over 45% can result in increased NO_x formation, because the excess nitrogen and oxygen in the combustion air entering the flame combine to form thermal NO_x. Firing with low excess air means limiting the amount of excess air that enters the combustion process, thus limiting the amount of extra nitrogen and oxygen entering the flame. Burner design modification accomplishes this and optimization uses oxygen trim controls. LEAF typically results in overall NO_x reductions of 5% to 10% when firing with natural gas, and is suitable for most boilers.

4. Low Nitrogen Fuel Oil

NO_x formed by fuel-bound nitrogen can account for 20% to 50% of total NO_x levels in oil-fired boiler emissions. The use of low nitrogen fuels in boilers firing distillate oils is one method of reducing NO_x emissions. Such fuels can contain up to 20 times less fuel-bound nitrogen than standard No. 2 oils. NO_x reductions of up to 70% over NO_x emissions from standard No. 2 oils have been achieved in firetube boilers utilizing flue gas recirculation.

5. Burner Modifications

Modifying the design of standard burners to create a larger flame achieves lower flame temperatures and results in lower thermal NO_x formation. While

117

most boiler types and sizes can accommodate burner modifications, it is most effective for boilers firing natural gas and distillate fuel oils, with little effectiveness in heavy oil-fired boilers. Also, burner modifications must be complemented with other NO_x reduction methods, such as flue gas recirculation, to comply with the more stringent environmental regulations. Achieving low NO_x levels (30 ppm) through burner modification alone can adversely impact boiler operating parameters such as turndown, capacity, CO levels, and efficiency.

6. Water/Steam Injection

Injecting water or steam into the flame reduces flame temperature, lower thermal NO_x formation and overall NO_x emissions. However, under normal operating conditions, water or steam injection can lower boiler efficiency by 3% to 10%. Also, there is a practical limit to the amount that can be injected without causing condensation-related problems. This method is often employed in conjunction with other NO_x control techniques such as burner modifications or flue gas recirculation. When used with natural gas-fired boilers, water or steam injection can result in NO_x reduction of up to 80%, with lower reductions achievable in oil-fired boilers.

7. Post-Combustion Emissions Control

There are several types of exhaust gas treatment processes that are applicable to industrial boilers.

8. Selective Non-Catalytic Reduction (SNCR)

In boiler SNCR, a NO_x reducing agent such as ammonia or urea is injected into the boiler exhaust gases at a temperature in the range of 1,400 to 1,600 °F. The agent breaks down the NO_x in the exhaust gases into water and atmospheric nitrogen (N_2). While SNCR can reduce boiler NO_x emissions by up to 70%, it is difficult to apply to industrial boilers, because that they are modulate or cycle frequently in order to perform properly, the agent must be introduced at a specific flue gas temperature. The location of the exhaust gases at the necessary temperature is constantly changing in a cycling boiler.

9. Selective Catalytic Reduction (SCR)

This technology involves the injection of the reducing agent into the boiler exhaust gas in the presence of a catalyst. The catalyst allows the reducing agent to operate at lower exhaust temperatures than SNCR, in the 500 to 1,200 °F depending on the type of catalyst. NO_x reductions of up to 90% are achievable with SCR. The two agents used commercially are ammonia (NH_3 in anhydrous liquid form or aqueous solution) and aqueous urea. Urea decomposes in the hot exhaust gas and SCR reactor, releasing ammonia. Approximately 0.9 to 1.0 moles of ammonia is required per mole of NO_x at the SCR reactor inlet in order to achieve a NO_x reduction range of 80% to 90%.

8.3 Ash Removal

8.3.1 Ash Removal From the Furnace

Stoker-fired units and dry-ash pulverized-coal-fired units are designed so that the ash settles in hoppers from which it is removed for disposal. Some possible uses for this slag are land fill, road-base material, granular material, aggregate for use in concrete blocks and preformed concrete, asphalt mix-material, cinders for icy roads, insulation, and grit for sandblasting. Most of these uses are applied also to ash removed in dry form from stoker and pulverized-coal-fired furnaces.

8.3.2 Particulate Removal

To meet the objective of a clear stack, some form of particulate removal equipment is now generally required to remove the fly ash from flue gases and units where fuels are burned in suspension. Several types of particulate removal equipments are available. These may be classified as electrostatic precipitators, mechanical dust collectors, fabric filters and wet scrubbers. Fly ash removed by equipments of these types may be used for most of the applications listed for ash removed as slag.

1. Electrostatic Precipitators

Electrostatic precipitators produce an electric charge on the particles to be collected and then propel the charged particles by electrostatic forces to the collecting electrodes. The precipitator operation involves four basic steps.

(1) An intense discharging field is maintained between the discharge electrode and the collecting electrodes.

(2) The carrier gases are ionized by the intense discharging field. These gas ions, in turn, charge the entrained particles.

(3) The negatively charged particles, still in the presence of an electrostatic field, are attracted to the positively(grounded)charged collecting electrodes.

(4) The collected dust is discharged by rapping into storage hoppers.

The collection efficiency of the electrostatic precipitator is related to the time of particle exposure to the electrostatic field, the strength of the field, and the resistivity of the dust particle. An efficiency of 99% is obtained at a cost generally favorable in comparison with other types of equipment. Hence, as of 1970, a very high percentage of particulate removal units installed in commercial boiler plants are electrostatic precipitators.

2. Mechanical Collectors

The operation of mechanical collectors depends on exerting centrifugal force on the particles to be collected by introducing the dust-laden gas stream tangentially into the body of the collector. The particulate matter is thrown to the outside wall of the collector where it is removed. Mechanical collectors operate most effectively in the particle-size range above about 10 microns. Below 10 microns, the collection efficiency drops considerably below 90%. As efficiency requirements continue to increase. The use of mechanical collectors is expected to decline.

3. Fabric Filters

Fabric filters operate by trapping dust by impingement on the fine filters comprising the fabric. As the collection of dust continues, an accumulation of dust particles adheres to the fabric surface. The fabric filter obtains its maximum efficiency during this period of dust build-up. After a fixed operating period, the bags must be cleaned. Immediately after cleaning, the filtering effciency is reduced until the build-up of collected dust takes place.

The fabric filter can be applied in any process area where dry collection is desired and where the temperature and humidity of the gases to be handled do not impose limitations. At efficiencies of 99% and less, the fabric filter is generally not competitive with the electrostatic precipitator for boiler application. However, for particulate matter, efficiencies above 99% can be achieved with fabric filters, and applications in congested areas may increase.

4. Wet Scrubbers

Wet scrubbers remove dust from a gas stream by collecting it with a suitable liquid(Fig. 8-1).

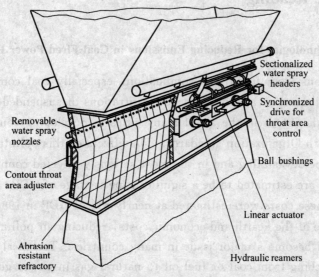

Sectionalized water spray headers

Synchronized drive for throat area control

Removable water spray nozzles

Ball bushings

Contout throat area adjuster

Linear actuator

Abrasion resistant refractory

Hydraulic reamers

Fig. 8-1   Venturi-type wet scrubber

A good wet scrubber is one that can effect the most intimate contact between the gas stream and liquid for the purpose of transferring the suspended particulate matter from the gas to the liquid. Collection efficiency, dust-particle size, and pressure drop are closely related in the operation of a wet scrubber. The required operating pressure drop varies inversely with the dust-particle size for a given collection efficiency; or a given dust-particle size for a given collection efficiency; or for a given dust-particle size, collection efficiency increases as operating pressure drop increases.

Unlike other particulate collection equipment, the wet scrubber employs a liquid stream to collect particulate matter. For this reason, it can usually perform additional process functions besides dust collection, Such as gas absorption, chemical reaction, and heat transfer. Simultaneous removal of dust and gaseous pollutants by use of a suitable scrubbing liquid can be accomplished with a wet scrubber.

121

Extensive Reading

Technologies for Reducing Emissions in Coal-Fired Power Plants

Emissions from fossil fuel combustion, especially coal combustion, are major contributors to air pollution. Concentrations of suspended particles and sulfur dioxide (SO_2) in the air of many cities in developing countries exceed World Health Organization standards. The effects of this pollution on human health can be devastating and in the most seriously affected countries the economic costs are estimated to be a significant percentage of GDP. In China, for instance, these costs were estimated at nearly 8% of GDP in 1995.

Because of the health and economic costs, reducing air pollution from fossil fuels has become a major issue in many countries. Technical solutions include: switching from coal or fuel oil to natural gas in power generation, increased use of renewable energy sources, energy efficiency measures, coal washing, vehicle standards and transport fuel reformulation. In addition, programs that implement clean coal technology in power generation, can significantly and quickly reduce air pollution.

Clean coal technologies are an especially important option for reducing hazardous fossil fuel emissions and, in developing countries where coal is readily available, are often a cost-effective option. Currently, several clean coal technologies are in different stages of development and commercialization. Market competition has resulted in steep cost declines, so technologies that were considered prohibitively expensive five years ago are now being used commercially. As a result, technologies once deployed only in industrial countries have now started to penetrate markets in developing countries.

This paper presents an update of the most important technologies for reducing fossil fuel emissions at power stations, including technology readiness and costs. It covers conventional technologies, cleaner and more efficient technologies, and advanced power generation

Conventional Technology

One conventional technology with wide application is the subcritical pulverized coal-fired power plant, with electrostatic precipitator for particulate emission control. The subcritical steam conditions (typically 16 MPa of main steam pressure, 538 ℃/566 ℃ of main steam temperature, and 538 ℃ or 566 ℃ of reheat steam temperature) are well suited to coal-fired power plants in the range of 300～600 MW. Smaller units (100～200 MW) use lower pressure. Larger units (500～600 MW) can be built for either subcritical or supercritical steam conditions. Local venders in China and India can currently supply subcritical but not supercritical units. Given current market conditions, local vendors can usually supply plants more cheaply than international competitors. The capital cost of a subcritical plant is estimated at US($ 1,000/kW) at international market prices, although the price could be lower($ 800/kW) in China or India.

Cleaner and More Efficient Technologies

Several cleaner technologies are available now in indeveloped countries for commercial application, and will be commercially available from now to 2020 in developing countries. These include supercritical steam units for pulverized coal-fired power plants, high efficiency electrostatic precipitators, flue gas desulferization processes, combustion modification and selective catalytic reduction (SCR), and atmospheric fluidized-bed combustion (AFBC).

Supercritical Steam Units

Supercritical steam conditions have been applied in large power plants (typically larger than 500 MW) in Europe, Japan, and the United States for the past quarter century. Early units were often unreliable especially in the case of the pressurized draft furnaces, most of these have since been converted to balanced draft furnaces. Staff at the plants were unfamiliar with the new materials and designs. But later supercritical steam units now have a track record of more than 20 years of reliable service.

Supercritical units have the same or better availability and the same or lower forced outage rates than subcritical plants. They are also more efficient and use significantly less fuel to produce the same amount of electricity. Plants using supercritical technology are 2%～5% more efficient than plants using subcritical technology. Supercritical technology also shows enormous potential for reducing greenhouse gasses and other emissions as well as fuel saving.

Standard supercritical steam conditions are 24 MPa of main steam pressure, 538 ℃/566 ℃ of main steam temperature, and 538 ℃/566 ℃ of reheat temperature. Recent improvements in materials and designs allow commercial plants to apply elevated steam temperatures (593 ℃/600 ℃), using ferritic steel to improve efficiency by another 2%～5%. However, developing countries need to introduce standard supercritical conditions and train operation and maintenance staff in standard supercritical technology before using elevated temperatures. Supercritical units with the same steam temperature will have the same fireside temperatures, and the steam conditions will not affect the fireside ash slagging or fouling characteristics. When the temperature is increased beyond 650 ℃, austenitic steel must be used—a difficult process that should be placed in a different category of advanced clean coal technology.

Supercritical technology needs to be made more readily available. One way to enable its use is to ensure that local markets are fully functional, so that the price of the units for local suppliers reflects international prices. Another is to promote technology transfers to local venders. The capital costs of the supercritical boiler and turbine will be 2%～5% higher than those of subcritical technology because the pressure parts of the supercritical unit are thicker. But since it improves efficiency and reduces plant size, the total capital costs of the unit will be only slightly higher than for subcritical units.

The high-efficiency Electrostatic Precipitator (ESP) for Particulate Control

Since coal typically contains 10%～20% ash, flue gas contains particulates that must be collected before the gases are emitted. The electrostatic precipitator (ESP) is the most commonly used collection technology for electrical power utilities, but in China the wet scrubber is used with smaller units (200 MW or less). The wet scrubber has less collecting efficiency than the ESP (below 96%) and does not meet the guidelines set by the World Bank (50 mg/Nm^3) as a primary measure of particulate control. But when the wet scrubber is installed as a measure to control SO_2 and as an auxiliary to the ESP particulate control, overall efficiency rises and particulate emissions fall.

The electric resistivity of ash affects the performance of ESP. Moisture, sulfur, sodium, and potassium reduce this resistance and are favorable to ash collection in ESP. On the other hand, calcium and magnesium hamper ash collection increase outlet emissions. Several steps can be taken to counter the problem associated with high resistivity ash and maintain performance at acceptable levels. These include intermittent charges; pulse charges; conditioning the flue gas with moisture, sulfur, or ammonium injection; and increasing the size of the ESP by widening the plate space.

The capital cost of ESP technology is around 5% of the total plant or between \$ 40~50/kW. Chinese manufacturers can provide the technology at \$ 15/kW, but these units do not meet the recommended level of 50 mg/Nm³. Cost-effective technologies for improving the collection of particulate emissions need to be transferred to developing countries.

Flue Gas Desulfurization for SO₂ Control

After particulates, SO_2 is usually the next target in reducing polluting emissions. Flue gas desulfurization (FGD) is a well-established method of removing SO_2 from flue gas and has been widely used in electric utility plants in Europe, Japan, and the United States since the 1970s. The technology therefore has a long history and has been fine-tuned to optimize performance. New and simplified FGD technologies have been proposed and demonstrated in China and other developing countries.

The limestone-gypsum type of FGD is widely used, because affordable limestone is readily available at many locations throughout the world. Limestone is converted into gypsum by absorbing SO_2 from flue gas. Gypsum can be used as a wall board or can be sold as a byproduct where such demand exists.

With the recent development of competitive markets and new technologies, the auxiliary power consumption and costs of FGD systems have been drastically reduced. FGD systems used to consume 3% or more of a plant's auxiliary power but now can operate on as little as 1%~1.5%. Five years ago the cost of an FGD system was reported at \$ 150~200/kW, but today that cost has fallen to \$ 70~120/kW.

Combustion Modification and Selective Catalytic Reduction to Control Nitrogen Oxide

Coal-fired power stations also generate nitrogen oxide (NO_x). Unlike particulate and SO_2 emissions, NO_x emissions are affected by the combustion process as well as the quality of the coal. Modifying the combustion process by optimizing the air flow from the burner can reduce NO_x emissions by 20%～30% at a relatively low cost ($5～10/kW). This low-cost option is the first that should be applied in existing plants. Two stage combustion and a low-NO_x burner are the next step in further reducing these emissions and can sometimes result in a 40%～60% decline in NO_x. These technologies are also relatively cheap to apply to new units ($5～10/kW), and the cost is modest ($10～20/kW) when they are applied to existing units.

Selective catalytic reduction (SCR) is a well-established approach to further reducing NO_x emissions. It typically reduces these emissions by 80%, at a cost of $40～80/kW. Because SCR has been applied to commercial plants in Europe and Japan since the 1980s, it has over 15 years of successful operating experience. The operation and maintenance processes have been established, including slip ammonium control and catalyst life estimation.

Atmospheric Fluidized-bed Combustion

Atmospheric fluidized-bed combustion (AFBC) has been widely applied to use low-grade coal or waste (opportunity fuel) at electric utility plants in the United States, Europe, and Japan since the 1980s. Hundreds of commercial plants are now in operation. The maximum unit size has been limited to around 200 MW, but a few 350 MW units have been built in Japan and France.

AFBC can remove SO_2 during the combustion process when limestone is used with the fuel. Because the combustion temperature is lower (850 ℃) with this technology, it generates relatively low NO_x emissions. Particulate emissions are controlled either by ESP or bagfilter.

The capital costs of AFBC are estimated at $1,000～1,300/kW, a competitive price when SO_2 control is required and low-grade fuel is available.

Advanced Power Generation

These relatively new technologies need to be more widely demonstrated, as they have the potential to reduce a number of emissions, including greenhouse gasses significantly. They should be commercially available in developing countries after 2010. The two most important are the pressurized fluidized bed combustion combined cycle (PFBC) and the integrated coal gasification combined cycle (IGCC).

126

New Words and Expressions

ash *n.*	灰
suspension *n.*	悬浮，暂停
disposal *n.*	丢掉，处理，布置
scrubber *n.*	洗涤塔
precipitator *n.*	除尘器，聚尘器
ionize *v.*	使离子化
rap *v.*	叩击，敲击
tangential *a.*	正切的，切线方向的
decline *v.*	拒绝，倾斜，跌落
trap *v.*	用陷阱捕捉，诱捕
humidity *n.*	湿气，潮湿，湿度
FGD(flue gas desulferization)	烟气脱硫
sulphate *n.*	硫酸盐
electrostatic precipitator	电除尘器
IDF (induced draft fan)	引风机

参 考 文 献

[1] Francis F. Huang. Engineering thermodynamics fundamentals and applications[M]. New York：Macmillan, 1976.

[2] Frank P. Incropera, David P. DeWitt. Introduction to heat transfer[M]. New York：Wiley, 1985.

[3] Feng Junkai. Notes of Steam Boiler Design[M]. Beijing：Tsinghua University,1992.

[4] J. R. GRACE. Circulating Fluidized Beds[M]. London：Blackie Academic and Professional, 1997.

[5] 李瑞扬. 热能与动力工程专业英语[M]. 黑龙江：哈尔滨工业大学出版社，2004.

[6] 阎维平. 热能与动力工程专业英语[M]. 北京：中国电力出版社,2005.

[7] 卜玉坤. 能源动力英语[M]. 北京：外语教学与研究出版社,2002.